SONG FOR THE UNRAVELING OF THE WORLD

SONG FOR THE UNRAVELING OF THE WORLD

Stories

Brian Evenson

COFFEE HOUSE PRESS
Minneapolis
2019

Coffee House Press books are available to the trade through our primary distributor, Consortium Book Sales & Distribution, cbsd.com or (800) 283-3572. For personal orders, catalogs, or other information, write to info@coffeehousepress.org.

Coffee House Press is a nonprofit literary publishing house. Support from private foundations, corporate giving programs, government programs, and generous individuals helps make the publication of our books possible. We gratefully acknowledge their support in detail in the back of this book.

LIBRARY OF CONGRESS CATALOGING-IN-PUBLICATION DATA

Names: Evenson, Brian, 1966– author.
Title: Song for the unraveling of the world / Brian Evenson.
Description: Minneapolis : Coffee House Press, 2019.
Identifiers: LCCN 2018040982 (print) | LCCN 2018043899 (ebook) |
    ISBN 9781566895569 (ebook) | ISBN 9781566895484 (trade pbk.)
Classification: LCC PS3555.V326 (ebook) | LCC PS3555.V326 A6 2019 (print) |
    DDC 813/.54—dc23
LC record available at https://lccn.loc.gov/2018040982

PRINTED IN THE UNITED STATES OF AMERICA

30 29 28 27 26 25 24 23   10 11 12 13 14 15 16

For Max,
but later
(only once you're as
tall as your lemon tree,
in stockinged feet)

&

For Kristen
stockinged or shod or barefoot
Then and Now and Always

The world itself withdraws like a tide,
uncovering a widening gap
which consciousness unfolds to fill . . .
—David Winters

CONTENTS

SONG FOR THE UNRAVELING OF THE WORLD

No Matter Which Way We Turned

No matter which way we turned the girl, she didn't have a face. There was hair in front and hair in the back—only saying which was the front and which was the back was impossible. I got Jim Slip to look on one side and I looked from the other and the other members of the lodge tried to hold her gently or not so gently in place, but no matter how we looked or held her, the face just wasn't there. Her mother was screaming, blaming us, but what could we do about it? We were not to blame. There was nothing we could have done.

It was Verl Kramm who got the idea of calling out to the sky, calling out after the lights as they receded, to tell them to come and take her. *You've taken half of her,* he shouted. *You've taken the same half of her twice. Now goddamn have the decency to take the rest of her.*

Some of the others joined in, but they didn't come back, none of them. They left, and left us with a girl who, no matter how you looked at her, you saw her from the back. She didn't eat, or if she did, did so in a way we couldn't see. She just kept turning in circles, walking backward and knocking into things, trying to grab things with the backs of her hands. She was a whole girl made of two half girls, but wrongly made, of two of the same halves.

After a while we couldn't hardly bear to look at her. In the end we couldn't think what to do with her except leave her. At first, her mother protested and bit and clawed, but in the end she didn't want to take her either—she just wanted to feel better about letting her go, to have the blame rest on us.

We nailed planks across the door and boarded up the windows. At Verl's request, we left the hole in the roof in the hope they would come back for her. For a while we posted a sentry outside the door, who reported to the lodge on the sound of her scrabbling within, but once the noise stopped we gave that up as well.

Late at night, I dreamed of her, not the doubled half of the girl we had, but the doubled half we didn't. I saw her, miles above us, in air rarefied and thin, not breathable by common means at all, floating within their vessel. There she was, a girl who, no matter where you turned, always faced you. A girl who bared her teeth and stared, stared.

Born Stillborn

Haupt's therapist had started coming to him at night as well, and even though Haupt knew, or at least suspected, that the man wasn't really there, wasn't really standing beside his bed with pencil in hand, listening to him and writing notes on the wall about what he said, he seemed real. There was writing on the wall when Haupt awoke. He could not read it but, being familiar with his therapist's unruly scrawl, its illegibility struck him as proving nothing. Their nighttime sessions felt, when he was honest with himself, just as real as his daytime sessions felt. Maybe even more real.

He did not report this to his therapist during the day. Instead, he waited to see if the therapist would mention it, and when he did not, decided that it must be some sort of test. No, as with so many other things, he would not share this with his therapist unless he was asked about it directly.

But during the day the therapist rarely asked about anything directly. He might say, "How was your week?" or "Did you have any dreams?" He was never more specific than that. At night, however, standing beside the bed, the night therapist would ask pointed questions, questions that wormed under his skin. When Haupt lied to him, he would say, "How gullible do you think I am?" When Haupt told only part of the truth, the night therapist would wait, tapping his pencil against the wall, for him to go on. And Haupt, at night, usually did go on, slowly extruding more and more of the truth through his mouth. It was as if the therapist was one thing at night and quite another during the day. Or even, it occurred to him, as if there were two of him, two different therapists who, for some reason, looked identical.

"Are you a twin?" asked Haupt once during a daytime session.

And the day therapist, usually reticent to talk about himself, was sufficiently caught off guard to say, "Yes," and then, shortly after, "No."

"Yes and no?" said Haupt. "How can it be both?"

"I . . . had a twin. He was born stillborn."

But when Haupt tried to question him more about it, the therapist shook his head. "We're here to talk about *you*," he claimed.

Born stillborn, Haupt thought now, late at night. What an odd way to phrase it, considering that in fact what you were saying was he wasn't born at all. Why not just say, *He was stillborn*? How was *born stillborn* different from simply *stillborn*? What had the day therapist been trying to tell him?

The night therapist was there beside him in the darkness, tapping his pencil against the wall, wanting something. What was it again? What had the man asked?

"I'm sorry," Haupt said. "My mind was elsewhere. What was the question again?"

The pencil stopped tapping. "Elsewhere," the night therapist said. "Where would that be?"

"Nowhere," Haupt lied.

The night therapist made a disgusted noise. "The mind's always somewhere," he said.

"I was thinking about something," Haupt admitted.

"About what?"

Haupt hesitated, trying to find a suitable lie. But the tapping of the pencil against the wall kept interrupting his thoughts, creating blinding little bursts of light in the darkness of his skull.

"I don't want to tell you," he finally said.

The tapping of the pencil stopped. Suddenly Haupt's head was dark again. "There," said the night therapist. "Now we're finally getting somewhere."

"Did you have any dreams?" his day therapist asked. They were sitting in his office, the chairs arranged as if for a staring contest. The day therapist wore glasses. This, Haupt felt, gave him an advantage. Did the night therapist wear glasses? He must, since the day therapist did, but Haupt didn't remember for certain. With the day therapist right there in front of him, he had a hard time imagining the night therapist.

"No dreams," Haupt said. And then he said, "I must have had some dreams." And then, "I'll be damned if I can remember them."

Damned, he thought, wincing inside. *Interesting choice of words.*

But his day therapist merely tented his fingers and nodded.

"How is an apple like a banana?" asked his night therapist a few nights later. The man had run out of space to write on one wall beside the bed so had moved closer to the window. There, in the cold glow of the streetlamp, he looked exceptionally pale, as if he had been chiseled from ice.

"Excuse me?" said Haupt.

"You heard me," the night therapist said. "Don't pretend you didn't."

"How do you know if I heard you or not?" he asked, irritated.

But the night therapist did not bother to answer.

"How is an apple like a banana?" Haupt mused. "They're both fruits," he said.

The therapist turned from the window and smiled. "Wrong," he said.

"Wrong?"

"They both have skin."

"Why is that a better answer than that they're both fruits?"

The therapist didn't say anything, just scribbled madly on the wall.

"What are you writing?" asked Haupt, but the man didn't answer.

"Why is yours the better answer?" Haupt insisted, but the man simply said, "The answer is, they both have skin."

The therapist can't possibly be there at night, Haupt thought near dawn, finding himself alone. *It doesn't make any sense. And besides, I didn't give him a key.* And yet the man looked exactly like his therapist. He spoke in a cadence exactly like his therapist's. If it wasn't his therapist, who else could he be?

He rubbed his eyes. *What else has skin?* he wondered idly. And then thought, *I do.*

He was like a banana and he was like an apple. If you were to draw a circle and put an apple and a banana in it, he would also be allowed to step into the circle. Nobody could stop him. Who was out there doing that, drawing circles around fruit, drawing circles around people?

He considered the chalk outlines that were drawn around dead bodies. So, it didn't have to be a circle exactly. Just a shape that could contain a fruit or a human or some combination of both.

During a lull in the conversation, he asked his day therapist what it was like to know you had been born a twin but would never meet your twin.

"Excuse me?" said the day therapist.

"You don't have to talk about it if you don't want to," said Haupt, using a phrase he'd often heard his day therapist use, usually at moments when Haupt suspected the man least meant it.

"How would I know what it's like to have a twin?" asked the day therapist.

"But," said Haupt, and stopped. "Weren't you . . . Didn't your twin brother . . . Wasn't he born stillborn?"

But the day therapist was shaking his head. "What twin brother? I was an only child."

Hadn't the day therapist told him he'd had a twin brother born stillborn? Haupt remembered the conversation nearly perfectly. There had been no possibility of misunderstanding his words. Why was his day therapist lying to him now?

He bought an apple. He ate it slowly, puncturing the skin with his teeth and chewing the skin up along with the rest of the apple, except for the seeds and pith. An apple wasn't like a banana, he thought. His night therapist was wrong. They both had skin, but with an apple you could eat the skin, and with a banana you couldn't. You could peel a banana easily with your fingers; an apple you couldn't. To peel an apple of its skin, you needed a knife. A person was more like an apple than a banana. You couldn't peel a person easily with your fingers. With a person, you needed a knife. With a person, like an apple, you could eat the skin.

He told this to his night therapist, but the man just stood at the window, motionless, not even writing. Haupt couldn't tell if the man was paying attention. He finished speaking and then waited, but the night therapist didn't turn his pale face away from the window.

"What's out there?" asked Haupt.

"What's out there?" echoed the night therapist, turning abruptly to look at him. "The whole world is out there."

But what, wondered Haupt, was the whole world? What did that even mean? If you were to draw a circle that contained the world, what else would belong within that circle? And where would you even draw it?

"What were you thinking about just then?" asked the night therapist. He was looking at Haupt now, eyes hungry, gaze steady. Haupt, unable under such a gaze to come up with a suitable lie, chose instead to try to change the subject.

It had never worked before, changing the subject. Not with the night therapist. There was no reason to think it would this time. The question Haupt asked wasn't a question he'd planned to ask—or would have asked if he had had time to think it over. It was simply the question that was lingering, unanswered, there within his skull. "What was it like being a twin but knowing you would never meet your twin?"

The therapist stopped, held himself very still. "How," he said slowly, "did you know I was born a twin?"

The world is a strange place, thought Haupt, alone in the dark, *almost unbearably so. And yet, it is the only place I have. And I'm not even entirely sure I have it.*

Why would the day therapist first admit he had a twin and then lie and pretend he did not? What sort of game was the man playing?

Suddenly, he knew the night therapist was there. Haupt drew the blankets judiciously up to his neck. He could see the therapist standing near the window, pencil poised.

"Shall we continue where we left off last time?" the night therapist asked.

Haupt shook his head, and then, worried that the gesture wouldn't be seen in the darkness, said, "No."

"No?"

"Who are you really?" asked Haupt.

"What do you mean?" asked the therapist. He turned to look at Haupt and again Haupt was struck by the paleness of the man's face.

"Were you born stillborn?" asked Haupt.

"Born stillborn?" asked the therapist slowly. And then his mouth stretched into a wide, mirthless smile. "What a curious way to put it," he said, in a kind of wonder.

"Would I need a knife to peel you?" Haupt asked.

That same mirthless smile, even wider now. "Why don't you find out?"

Haupt threw back the covers. Underneath, he was wearing his clothing. He had been wearing his clothing all night. He approached his therapist, knife in his white-knuckled hand, but the therapist did not move.

He lunged with the knife, but he must have closed his eyes briefly, for the therapist wasn't quite where Haupt thought he was, and was unscathed. He lunged again, and this time saw the knife pass through the therapist's chest effortlessly, as if it wasn't there at all. But when he looked up at the man's face, he found his mouth to be full of blood.

The man laughed, and the blood spilled down his chin. Haupt pushed the knife through him again and more blood came out of the man's mouth but there was still no sign of a wound on his body, still no feel of resistance as the knife went in.

"What's wrong with you?" asked Haupt, alarmed.

"What's wrong with *me*?" said the therapist. "How can I answer that? Don't you know by now that our time is supposed to be about you? Haupt, what's wrong with *you*?"

Time passed. At some point, Haupt dropped the knife and made for the door. But there was the night therapist, just in front of him, no matter which way he turned. Haupt, more and more confused, had felt parts of his mind growing numb, shutting down. *What sort of treatment is this?* one of the remaining parts of his mind wondered. *Isn't this sort of thing frowned upon by the therapeutic community?* But when he asked the therapist, the man simply laughed and came closer. *Shouldn't I have been given a safe word?* another part of him wondered.

"A safe word?" said the therapist, though Haupt was certain that he hadn't vocalized the thought. "Has anything I've done suggested that this was a game of any sort, let alone one of a sexual nature?"

"Are you alive?" asked Haupt.

"Are you?"

"What are you?" asked Haupt.

"What am I? I'm exactly what you think I am."

And when Haupt's mind turned inward, trying to understand what he thought the therapist to be, the man moved closer, licking his bloody lips.

He woke up in the morning on the floor, sore. There were shallow cuts on his hand, and his lips, though uncut, were black with blood. With a groan, he got up and picked up the knife. He took a shower.

He would talk to his day therapist, he told himself. He would confront the man. He would ask why he was coming at night. And if he wasn't coming at night, if all of it was his imagination or something much worse, well, then at least he would know.

He ate an apple, then ate a banana. There was something wrong with the banana—it was harder to chew up than he remembered bananas being: it tasted stringy, bitter. But the apple tasted exactly like he remembered apples tasting. He chewed slowly, washing them both down with water.

"How was your week?" asked his day therapist.

"Fine," he said. He was hunched over, his hands in his jacket pockets, folded in on himself.

"Did you have any memorable dreams?" asked his day therapist, after a long silence.

"No," he claimed. "Not a one."

All the while he was thinking, *Born stillborn. Stillborn and yet born. What a terrible thing that must be. If a twin doesn't survive in the womb,* he was thinking, *it is usually because the other twin takes the nourishment meant for him. If that twin is stillborn, it's fine: he can be buried and forgotten and he will stay in the ground. But if a twin is* born *stillborn, well, where does that leave him exactly?*

His day therapist was staring at him. How long had he been staring? Perhaps a great deal of time had gone by.

"What is it?" asked Haupt.

"What were you thinking about just then?" asked the therapist. Behind the lenses of his glasses, his eyes looked attentive, alert.

"This and that," Haupt said.

His day therapist stayed still, waiting him out, more like the night therapist than the day therapist. Again Haupt wondered whether he should think of them as one person, or two.

The day therapist was still staring at him. Haupt moved his hands within his pockets until one of them found the handle of the knife and closed over it. He squeezed it.

"I was thinking about apples," he said.

"Apples?" said the day therapist, surprised.

"And bananas," said Haupt. "What do you suppose apples and bananas have in common?"

The day therapist's eyes narrowed slightly. "Is this a trick question?" he asked.

"Of course it is," said Haupt. He imagined his knuckles going white around the handle of the knife. The day therapist was more like an apple than a banana. He would not be easy to peel. Perhaps it would be better to chew all of him up. "But answer it anyway," Haupt said. "Humor me."

Leaking Out

It was abandoned, the clapboard peeling and splintered, but practically a mansion. And surely, thought Lars, warmer than the outside. No wind, at least. The front door was padlocked and the windows boarded, but it didn't take long to find the place where the boards only looked nailed down and the shards of glass had been picked out of a window frame. The place where, with a minimum of effort, he could wriggle his way through and inside.

But of course that place meant that someone had arrived before him, and might still be inside. *He* didn't mind sharing—it was a big enough house that there was plenty of it to go around—but would *they*?

"Hello?" he called softly into the darkened house. When there was no answer, he pushed his duffel bag through the gap and wormed in after it.

He waited for his eyes to adjust. Even after a few minutes had passed all he saw were odd thin gray stripes floating in the air around him. Eventually, he divined these to be the joins between the boards nailed over the windows, letting the slightest hint of light leak in.

He felt around with one gloved hand. The floor seemed bare. No rubbish, no sign of habitation—which meant that whoever had been here hadn't stayed long or perhaps, like him, had just arrived.

"Hello?" he called again, louder this time, then listened. No answer.

Just me, then, he told himself. Though he wasn't entirely sure it *was* just him. He groped for the top of his duffel bag and unzipped it, then worked his glove off with his teeth so he could root around by touch inside. Lumps of cloth that were wadded dirty clothing, the squat cylinders of batteries, the thin length of a knife, a dented tin plate, a can of food, another. There it was, deep in the bag: a hard, long cylinder with a pebbled grip. He took it out, fiddled with it until he found the switch.

The flashlight beam came on, the glow low, the battery nearly dead or the contacts corroded. He shook the flashlight a little and its beam brightened enough to cut through the dark.

He shined it about him, walking around. Ordinary room, it seemed. The only odd thing was how clean it was: no debris, no dust. The pine floors shone as if they had just been waxed. Immaculate. Had he been wrong in thinking the house deserted? But no, it had appeared ruined from the outside, and the windows were boarded.

Strange, he thought. And then the flashlight flickered and went out.

He shook it, slapped it with the heel of his hand, but it didn't come on again. He cursed himself for having left his duffel bag near the window. He retreated slowly backward in what he hoped was the direction he had come from. Darkness was making the space change, become uncertain, vast. He kept backing up anyway.

The backstay of his shoe struck something. Feeling behind him he found a wall. Where was the window he had entered through? He couldn't find it, there was just solid wall.

It's only a house, he told himself. *No need to worry. Only a house.*

But he'd never been able to bear the dark. He hadn't liked it when he was a boy and he didn't like it now. He felt along the wall again. Still no window. He was hyperventilating, he realized. *Take a breath,* he told himself, *calm down.*

He passed out.

When he woke up he was calm somehow, as if he were another person. He had none of the disorientation that comes from waking in a strange place. It was almost as if the place wasn't strange after all—as if he'd been there a very long time, perhaps forever.

The stripes, he thought. And immediately he began to see them, the lines of gray that marked the windows. There were none near him—the wall he had been touching must have been an interior wall, he must have taken a wrong turn somewhere. How had he gotten so turned around?

He stood and made his way to them. Halfway there, he stumbled over something and went down in a heap. His duffel bag, he thought at first, but when he groped around on the floor for it, he found nothing at all. What had he tripped on?

He climbed to his feet. Once he touched the wall with the window in it, he swept his foot over the floor looking for his duffel bag, but still didn't find it. He tugged on the slats of wood over the window. None were loose.

Wrong window, he thought, *wrong wall.* He did his best not to panic.

Turning away, he peered into the darkness. He could barely make out, at what seemed a great distance, another set of lines defining another set of windows. He made his way toward it.

The duffel bag was there this time—he stumbled on it, and when he bent down and felt around for it, it had the decency not to vanish. It felt slightly wrong beneath his fingers. No doubt that had come about when he had forced it through the gap in the boards and let it drop. He shouldn't worry, it was his duffel bag: what else could it possibly be?

Sitting cross-legged on the floor, he searched through it for the spare batteries and in a moment had them. He unscrewed the cap at the end of the flashlight. Shaking out the old batteries, he dropped them onto the floor with a thunk and then pushed the new ones in, screwing the cap back into place.

Carefully he pressed the switch, and this time the beam came on bright and strong. The room became a room again, boundaries clear and distinct. Nothing to be afraid of, just an ordinary room, empty except for him and his duffel bag.

He slung the bag over his shoulder and started toward the door that led deeper into the house. Halfway there he stopped and, turning, swept the light across the floor behind him. *The dead batteries,* he wondered, *where can they possibly have gone?* They simply weren't there.

The adjoining room offered a stairway and then narrowed into a passageway that led to the remainder of the ground floor. Here too everything appeared immaculate, the floor and stairs dustless, as if they had just been cleaned.

He shined the light up the stairway but didn't climb it, instead following the passage back. After openings leading to a dining room, a kitchen, and a storeroom, the passage terminated in a series of three doors, one directly before him and one to either side. He tried the door to his right and found it locked. The one on the left was locked as well. But the door in front of him opened smoothly. He went through.

A fireplace dominated the room, a large ornate affair faced in porcelain tile. The grate and firebox were as clean as the rest of the house: spotless, as if a fire had never been made. There was a perfectly symmetrical stack of wood to one side, a box of kindling in front of it. On the other side was a poker in its stand, also seemingly unused. The porcelain of the tiles had been painted with what at first struck him as birds but which, as he drew closer, he realized were not birds at all but a series of gesticulating disembodied hands.

And there, on the wall above the mantel, what he took at first for a curious work of art: something seemingly scribbled directly on the plaster. Upon closer inspection, it proved to be a stain—the only blemish he had seen in the whole house. And then he came closer, and closer still, and recoiled: it was not just any stain, he realized. It was the remnants of a great cloud of blood.

There were two armchairs here and a bearskin on the floor. He could light a fire and get warm. Did he dare start one? What if someone saw smoke coming up from the chimney? Would they cause trouble for him?

But his batteries wouldn't last forever and the last thing he wanted was to be left in the dark again. No, he needed a fire. If he was caught, so what: it would mean a night in jail and then they'd let him go. And the jail would be warm.

He balanced the flashlight on its end so that the light fountained up toward the ceiling, then rummaged through his bag until he found his book of matches.

It was bent and crumpled, the striking pad worn along the middle of the strip through to the paper backing. Most of the matches were torn out and gone.

Carefully he arranged the split logs in a crosshatched stack, and then on top of this built a little mound of tinder. The mound looked, he realized, like a star, and once he'd noticed this he found his fingers working to make it even more of one.

The first match he struck fizzled out. The second did a little better, but the tinder didn't catch. With the third, once the match was alight he ignited the matchbook as well, pushing both into the tinder.

He blew on the flame until the tinder caught, watched it blacken and curl, charring its mark onto the pale wood below, and then that caught too. He stared into the flames. Soon he felt the warmth radiating from the fire. Soon after that, it was too hot to stay near.

He made his way back to one of the armchairs. Before he could sit in it, he realized there was something already there. A rubberized blanket perhaps, strangely shaped and nearly see-through. An odd color, a dirty pink—pigskin maybe, stretched thin or perhaps cured in a way that gave it translucency. It was soft to the touch, and warm—no doubt from the fire. He grasped it in both hands and lifted it, found it to be more a sheath than a blanket, something you could crawl into, as large as a man, roughly the shape of a man as well.

He dropped it as if stung, took a few steps away from the chair. His first impulse was to flee, but with each step away from the sheath he felt safer, more secure. *Somebody's idea of a joke,* he told himself, *an odd costume.* Nothing to worry about.

He settled into the other chair, still shaken. He would rest for a few minutes, warm up, and then leave.

A moment later, he was sound asleep.

He dreamed that he was in an operating theater, much like the one his father had performed surgery in when he was still alive. There was a chair on the upper tier reserved solely for him, his name on a brass plate set in the back of the chair. When he entered the theater, everyone turned and faced him, and stared. It was crowded, every chair taken but his own, and to reach his spot he had to force his way down the aisle and to the center of the row, stepping with apologies over the legs of the others. Down below, the surgeon stood with his gloved hands held motionless and awkwardly raised, his face mostly hidden by his surgical mask. He seemed to be waiting for Lars to take his seat.

Lars sat and then, when the surgeon still continued to stare at him, motioned for him to proceed. The surgeon nodded sharply and turned toward the only other man on the theater floor: a tall, elderly gentleman, stripped nude and standing just beside the operating table.

The surgeon ran his hand across a tray of instruments and took up a scalpel. He made a continuous incision along the man's clavicle, from one shoulder to the other. The elderly man didn't seem to mind or even to feel it. He remained standing, smiling absently. The surgeon set the bloody scalpel down on the edge of the operating table. Carefully, he worked his gloved fingers into the incision he had created and then, once he had a firm grasp on the skin, began very slowly to pull it down, gradually stripping the man's flesh off his chest in a single slick sheet, from time to time looking back at Lars, as if for approval.

Lars awoke gasping, unsure of where he was. He was sweating, the room warmer than when he'd fallen asleep, the fire glowing a deep red, the heat making the air in front of the fireplace shimmer.

"Bad dream?" asked a voice.

He turned, startled. There in the other armchair was a man. Something was wrong with his skin: it hung strangely on him, too loose in the fingers and elbows, too tight in other places. There was something wrong too with his face, as if the skin didn't quite align with the bones beneath. One eye was oddly stretched so that it was open too wide, the other bunched and all but shut.

"Bad dream?" asked the malformed man again.

"Yes, it is," said Lars.

"*Was,* you mean," said the malformed man. But Lars had not meant *was* but *is. I'm dreaming,* thought Lars. *I'm still asleep and dreaming.*

"What are you staring at?" asked the man. "Is it me?" He reached up and touched his face, and then began to tug on it, sliding the skin slightly over with a wet sucking sound. The eye that had been bloated began to shrink back, the other eye opening up. Lars, sickened, had to look away.

"There we are," said the man. "You see? Nothing to be concerned over." When Lars still stared into the fire, he added, "Look at me."

Reluctantly Lars did. It was, he saw, just a normal man now, not malformed at all.

"What was wrong with you?" he couldn't stop himself from asking.

"Wrong?" asked the man. He smoothed back his hair. "Nothing. Why would you think anything is wrong?"

Lars opened his mouth, then closed it again. From the other chair, the man watched him.

"I hadn't realized someone else was here," Lars finally managed. "I didn't mean to intrude. I'll go."

"Nonsense," said the man. "It's a big house. A mansion of sorts. I don't mind sharing."

"It's only—"

"Don't worry," said the man. "I've already eaten."

What the hell? wondered Lars. Had the man thought he wasn't going to stay because he had no food to offer? Was that a custom around these parts? Confused, he started to rise from the chair.

But the other man was already up, patting the air in front of him with his hands. *Sit, sit,* he was saying. To get past him, Lars would have to touch him, and that was something he felt he did not want to do.

He let himself fall back into the chair. Impossibly, the man was already back at his own chair as well, sitting down. The skin on one side of his face seemed to be growing loose again, or maybe that was no more than the flickering of the firelight.

"I didn't mean to wake you," said the man. "Though perhaps it wasn't I who woke you."

"I . . . don't know," said Lars.

The man uncrossed his legs and then crossed them in the other direction. "Will you tell it to me?" he asked.

"Tell you what?"

"Your dream? Will you share it with me?"

"I don't think that's a good idea."

The man smiled, gave a little laugh. "No? Then the least I can do is try to help you fall back to sleep."

"There was once a man who was not a man," the man began. He was frowning—or perhaps it was that his face was slipping. "He acted like a man, and yet he was not in fact a man, after all. Then why, you might wonder, did he live with men or among them?

"Why indeed?

"But this is not that kind of story, the kind meant to explain things. It simply tells things as they are, and as you know there is no explanation for how things are, at least none that would make any difference and allow them to be something else.

"He acted like a man and in many respects he *was* a man, and yet he was not a man as well, and sometimes he would forget this and allow himself to relax a little and leak out."

"What?" said Lars, his voice rising.

"Leak out," said the man. He had pulled his chair a little closer, or at least it seemed that way to Lars.

"But what," said Lars, "how—"

"Leak out," said the man with finality. "I already told you this is not that kind of story, the kind that explains things. Be quiet and listen.

"He would relax a little and leak out, and sometimes it was hard for him to make his way back in again. Sometimes people would come along while he was this way, humans, and he'd have to decide what to do with them. Or perhaps *to* them. Sometimes, if he couldn't get back in to where he had been, he could at least get into one of them."

The man reached out abruptly and touched his cheek. Lars felt warmth spreading through his face. Or maybe it was cold, but so cold it felt warm. He found he could not move.

"Sometimes," said the man, "once he got into one of them, he would stay for a while. But other times, he would simply swallow them up and be done with them."

II.

When he woke up, it was late in the day, enough sunlight leaking through the gaps between boards to fill the house with a pale light. He was lying on the floor, on the bearskin, and had slept in such a way that he was stiff all along one side, his shoulder tingling, his jaw tight. The other man was nowhere to be seen.

Had anything really happened? Perhaps he had dreamed it all.

The ashes in the grate were still warm. The room, which had seemed to him so immaculate in his flashlight beam the night before, clearly wasn't: the floor was dusty. There was litter and garbage as well, and a faint sour smell. The bearskin he had slept on was moth-eaten and tattered, as were the two chairs. The only place that was immaculate was the wall above the fireplace: there wasn't a stain there after all.

He quickly packed his duffel bag and made for the door. He wouldn't come back, he told himself. He was, after all, just passing through. He'd never stayed in the same place more than a day or two, not since his father's death.

He searched the house, found nothing of value. The dead batteries still weren't anywhere.

It was late afternoon by the time he walked the half mile into town. The town was smaller than he'd hoped, the business district little more than one main street, with a diner, a general store with a lunch counter in back, a drugstore, a feed and grain supply, a hardware store. He spent some time in the hardware store. Unfortunately, there weren't enough other customers and the clerk was paying too much attention for him to lift anything. So he left and walked down to the general store.

He moved down the aisles, considering. One clerk here too, seemingly the identical twin of the fellow in the hardware store, albeit less attentive. In the candy aisle he slipped a pair of energy bars into his coat pocket as he bent down to pretend to examine something on the bottom shelf. Batteries were on an endcap and a little trickier to pocket unobserved. It took him some time to position his body between the display and the clerk in such a way as to allow him to surreptitiously slip a set down his pants.

He wandered a little more, to throw off the scent. By the time he was turning again toward the front of the store, prepared to leave without buying anything, it was beginning to grow dark outside, snow just starting to fall. The clerk seemed to have doubled, having been joined by his brother or cousin or whatever the fuck he was from the hardware store next door. Unless there was a third one floating around. They were whispering back and forth, watching him.

He briefly considered putting everything back. But he needed the food—it had been well over a day since he had had anything to eat—and he needed the batteries too, particularly if he was going to spend another night outdoors. He needed to be certain his flashlight wouldn't go out. *Matches, too,* he thought, *otherwise no fire.* He found a box of them, slipped them into his duffel bag.

The clerk from the hardware store was heading toward him, his lips a tight line. The other clerk, the one who actually worked there, had moved to block the front door.

Lars headed quickly up the aisle and toward the back of the store. Behind him, the man closest to him gave a shout, and Lars burst into a run, darting through the door marked *Employees Only.* He swerved around boxes and metal shelves until he reached the back wall. He chose a direction and ran along it until he hit the door, a metal bar slung about waist level. He pushed on the bar and the door opened to a blast of cold and an alarm went off. And then he was out in an alley, the light fading, snow drifting slowly down. He ran, his feet slipping on the ice, hearing the sounds of the two clerks in pursuit.

He ran until he no longer heard them, no longer felt them behind him. Then he stopped, listened. It was all but dark out now. He walked for a while, catching his breath. Where was he? He wasn't sure exactly—on one of the roads leading out of town, fields on all sides. And then he heard something, a cry from behind him. He began to run again.

And then in the darkness he heard voices even closer, as if he had not run away from the two men but toward them. He cut quickly off the road and into the field beside it—only it wasn't a field but a house and its grounds. Almost a mansion from what he could see of it. And then he realized exactly what house it was.

But he hadn't been anywhere near it. How could that house be here?

The voices drew closer. Would they see him if he stood motionless in the house's yard? It was already dark, but was it dark enough? Would his face shine like a buoy in the darkness?

It's only a house, he tried to tell himself. *Only an ordinary house. Nothing to worry about.* Before the voices came any closer, he forced himself to walk toward it, find the loose boards covering the window, and squirm in.

Later, he wondered if he had heard voices after all. Or, rather, wondered if the voices he had heard had been connected to the two clerks, if they were still chasing him. That was, he told himself as he waited in the house, the heart of the matter. Either the voices were the clerks' or they weren't. But if they weren't, whose were they?

I'll just wait a little, he told himself once inside, *just until I'm sure they're gone.* But each time he thought he was safe and made for the window, he heard them again. Or heard something like them, anyway.

How much time passed? He wasn't sure. Had he slept? He didn't think so, although it was much darker in the house now, so dark he couldn't see at all save for the pale lines marking the joins between the window boards.

He got out his flashlight. It wasn't wise, not if the two men were still outside looking for him, but he couldn't help himself—he couldn't stand the dark, not in here. He turned it on, pointed it at the ground.

The room, he saw, looked exactly as it had the night before: clean, immaculately so, the floor freshly polished. As if it were not a deserted house after all. Having the flashlight on made him feel better. But seeing the impossibly polished floor made him feel worse.

He listened. The voices came and went for a while and then dissolved into wind, a lonely sound with nothing human to it at all. He pulled on the boards to look out and see if they were still there—or tried to: the boards wouldn't give. It was as if they had been nailed back in place since he had entered. He pulled at them, hammered on them with his flashlight. Disoriented, he looked around, tried the boards on the other window. They were all tightly nailed in place.

He went to the front door, unlocked it, rattled the handle. It felt almost like something held the door shut from the other side. He hit it with his shoulder, hard, and then stopped. It had been padlocked, he remembered. Of course it wouldn't open.

All he needed was something to pry the boards away from the window. It didn't matter how they had gotten stuck—it was not worth thinking about. All that mattered was to get them off and get out.

But there was nothing in the room—the room was empty: he knew that already. He hit one of the boards with the butt of his flashlight. He stopped when its beam began to flicker. He couldn't bear to be without a light. Not here. He needed to find something he could pry with. He would have to find something else.

He traveled back and forth between the entrance hall and the hallway, always stopping shy of the door at the end of the hallway. He searched the kitchen, found nothing but empty cabinets. The dining room was empty too. He tried the doors to either side at the end of the passage, found them both still locked. He kept searching the same empty rooms and finding nothing. *I won't go,* he was telling himself. *Not in there.*

But in the end he did go in. In his mind he could see the poker, leaning in its stand right beside the fireplace. He could pry the boards off with it. He would rush in, take the poker, and leave. He would look at nothing, no one. He would think about nothing, no one. He would simply come and go. He wouldn't stay.

But when he finally opened the door, he found a fire already lit, roaring in the fireplace. He couldn't help but see that. And he couldn't help but see that spray of blood there again on the wall above the mantel, looking even larger than before. Just as he couldn't help but see the creature in the chair, struggling into, or perhaps out of, its skin. The skin was on the bottom half of its body, but not the top half.

It looked at him and perhaps smiled. Moved its face anyhow in a way that frightened him.

"Back for more?" it said.

"I was just leaving," said Lars.

The creature ignored him. "You wanted another story?" it said. "Is that what you came for?" And it reached out toward his face.

It didn't touch him, but his face still felt warm. He could not, he suddenly found, move.

It reached down and wormed further into the sheath. What had not been a hand became a hand. It flexed the fingers experimentally, settling the skin deeper around them.

"No story," it said. "I haven't eaten."

Lars felt the flashlight slip from his fingers. It struck the floor with a thunk and began to roll away, until the sound was abruptly cut off as if, suddenly, the flashlight was no longer there.

"Well," it said. "What am I to do with you?"

The fire roared and then without warning fell silent; the rest of the room, too. In the silence, the creature came closer. First it touched Lars with its hand, then with the thing that was not a hand, and finally it wrapped what remained of the loose, empty skin around him and drew him in.

Song for the Unraveling of the World

Drago thought what he was hearing was his daughter singing through the thin wall. He lay in the narrow bed listening to the sound of her voice, trying to make out the song's words. He could barely make out the melody, such as it was: off-key, meandering. He could make little sense of it. Soon, he was not so much listening as letting the sound lull him to sleep.

But when he awoke the next morning and went to wake her, his daughter was gone. There was no sign she had slept in the room; the bed was neatly made. The blanket she had kept with her ever since her arrival was folded in the center of the bed in a neat square. The bed had been pulled away from the wall, and the objects in the room—clothing, toys, souvenirs, oddments—had been meticulously arranged to form a circle around it. It was nearly a perfect circle: how had a five-year-old child managed that?

"Dani?" he called out, but there was no answer.

The door to her bedroom was locked from the outside, precisely as he had left it the night before. He thought she must be hiding somewhere in the room, and so pretended they were playing hide-and-seek.

"Where's Dani?" he said in too deep of a voice. "Here I come to get Dani!"

He waited for her giggling to give her away, but there was no giggling. She wasn't under the bed and she wasn't in the closet. Apart from those two places, there was no place in the room for her to hide.

He couldn't find her in the rest of the house either. Not in the kitchen, not in the laundry room, not in the living room. The bathrooms, too, were empty. He even looked in the basement, though he knew there was no way she would go down there willingly on her own. The front and back doors were still bolted shut and the windows all nailed shut as usual. Which meant she had to be in the house.

Only, she wasn't in the house.

He went through the house again, meticulously this time, looking even in places that were too small for her. He opened the refrigerator; she wasn't inside. Had she wedged herself behind it somehow? No. Had she somehow worked her way into the ventilation system? The vents' cover plates were all screwed firmly in place. Was she crammed into a drawer? But even on the third pass—when, heart beating hard in his throat, he was looking less for her than for bits and pieces of her, some remnant of her, something to prove she had once existed (peering in jars, looking in the dank space behind the water heater, shining a flashlight down the garbage disposal)—she still wasn't there.

He sat down on the couch, stared at the dead screen of the television. He wasn't sure what to do. She wasn't there. Yet there was no way she could *not* be there. He kept expecting her to pop out at any moment, kept expecting himself to think of one more place he hadn't thought to look—a neglected closet, some sort of semisecret room—and to find her there, curled in a tight ball, waiting for him.

Dully, he reached out and switched the television on. The channel was nothing but static. He reached to adjust the coat-hanger antenna on top of the console and then stopped. Maybe she was there, in the static, he thought absurdly. That was somewhere he hadn't checked. Maybe if he stared long enough, he would glimpse her.

His eyes hurt. He was not sure how much time had passed. An hour, maybe two. It took an effort for him to reach out again and switch the set off. Even after it was off, he stared for a long time at the small dot of light in the center of the curved gray-green screen, and then at the dead screen itself.

He had looked all through the house: she wasn't there. He could look again. Or accept that somehow, unlikely as it seemed, she had managed to make her way out.

As soon as this thought crossed his mind, he couldn't understand what had been wrong with him. He shouldn't still be sitting here. He should have gone out to look for her hours ago.

Next to his home was a single-story house of gray brick, rusted white metal awnings above the windows. The door he knocked on was peeling and left flakes of faded yellow paint on his knuckles. He rubbed the back of his hand against his shirt, waited.

He had to knock twice more before he heard footsteps and a clanking noise. A moment passed, then somebody opened the door. A bone-thin woman, probably midsixties, an oxygen cannula running into her nostrils. She kept the chain on the door, peering out through the gap.

"I'm looking for my daughter," Drago said.

The woman just shook her head. He heard the chirp of oxygen being propulsed through the cannula. "Mister," she said, "you come to the wrong house. I don't got anybody's daughter here."

He blocked the door with his foot before she could close it. "Let me explain," he said.

The woman tried a few times to close the door through his foot, then gave up. Lips tight, she waited.

He explained that his daughter had gone missing. He described her: blond hair, five years old, a curved scar on her left temple—

"How'd she get the scar?" the woman asked.

He shook his head impatiently. "That doesn't matter," he said. "Have you seen her?"

"Who are you again?" the woman asked.

He told her his name. Or, rather, not his actual name: the one he'd been living under. "Tom Smith. I live next door. You must have seen us move in a few months back."

"That's a weird name for a man with your accent," she said.

"I was adopted," he lied. "Tom Smith," he insisted.

All the time, chirp, chirp, chirp.

The woman shook her head. "I've seen through the windows a man moving around over there, next door. Could be you. But I ain't never seen no little girl."

"I'm always with her," Drago said. "If you saw me, you saw her, too."

"Don't you have a job?" she asked.

"That's not important," he said.

"I mean, what do you do with her when you're at work?"

"I . . . ," said Drago. "Please, have you seen her or not?" He was almost shouting it.

"I ain't never seen no little girl like the one as described," she said. "Not through the windows of that house over next door nor anywhere else near."

"O.K.," said Drago. He took a deep breath. "If you do see her, will you let me know?"

"Mister," the woman said, "you get a five-year-old missing in a neighborhood even half so bad as this one you don't go door to door letting on. What you got to do is call the police."

Thanking her, he quickly left.

In principle, Drago agreed with her. What any normal person would do in a situation like this was call the police. But he couldn't call the police. It just wasn't possible.

The neighbors on the other side weren't home. The house directly across the street was deserted, the windows boarded over, the façade tagged with red spray paint. The front door was firmly shut and locked. He circled around the house, blowing on his hands to keep them warm, pulling at the boards to make sure they were all firmly in place. Even though they were, it didn't mean anything: anyone with a door key could come and go, so he went around behind the house and kicked the back door in.

The house was dark inside, almost no light coming through the boarded-up windows. Using his phone as a flashlight, he walked through. It was deserted inside, no sign of squatters or habitation. He kept expecting to find his daughter's dead body as he moved from room to room, but he didn't find anything at all.

He went back out, closing the back door as best he could, then crossed the street and got into his car.

He drove slowly down the block, looking right and left, then did a u-turn and drove down it again. From there, he drove a rectangle around the block, then a larger rectangle around that, careful to drive down each and every street. He kept moving in wider and wider arcs, turning around his house, looking for his daughter, looking for Dani.

Late afternoon found him at a rundown bar a half mile away, showing a photograph of his daughter to a trio of hapless old men. It was the only photograph he had, and it was a year out of date, although it still looked like her more or less. The men kept shaking their heads, refusing to hold the photo, hardly even speaking.

He tried another bar, then another.

"Maybe you should come back later, when more people are here," said the bartender in the third one.

"Sure," Drago said. "But no harm in trying now, is there?"

The bartender nodded and stared at the picture again. "Who used to be in the other half of it?" he asked.

"Just me," lied Drago. "I tore that half off. I wanted people to focus on my daughter."

The bartender looked at him, looked back at the photo, looked at him again. "Doesn't look like your hand," he said. "Looks more like a woman's hand."

"I'm just trying to find my daughter," Drago said. When the bartender looked him in the eyes he met the man's gaze, held it until, at last, with a sigh, the fellow handed the photo back to him.

After that, he stopped going into bars. He just drove around for a while, hoping an idea would come to him, some sense of what might have happened, where she might have gone. But nothing came.

He drove through the downtown, didn't see her. He went into the McDonald's closest to their home, showed the photo around, a little more of it torn off now so no part of any adult she had been with was visible. She hadn't been in there either.

He drove past the bus station, then on impulse parked, went in. There were a few transients sleeping in the chairs, trying to escape the cold. She hadn't had a coat, he realized—her coat had formed part of the circle around her bed. If she were outside, she'd be very cold by now.

Besides the transients, a few other people nervously waited for a bus out of town, or waited on someone coming in. He checked the men's bathroom and had a woman coming out of the women's go back in and check there. He walked up and down the station, showed her photo to the clerk behind the glass. No luck.

He was finished, about to leave and continue his aimless driving, when he saw the payphone on the wall. He checked for change in his pockets and when he found he had enough, started toward it. At the last moment, he swerved away, went and sat on a chair.

It's a mistake to call, he told himself.

Yes, of course, but what else is there to do? I can't find her in the house, I can't find her in town, I can't go to the police. What am I supposed to do? Just wait until she shows up again?

But it's impossible that she is gone. I have the only key to the door and I still have it. No sign of forced entry. She should still be there.

You think if you go back, she'll have suddenly appeared again?

He shrugged. No, he didn't think that. The problem was, he didn't know what to think.

...

In the end, having no other options, he called. The phone rang three times, and when she did not answer, he hung up before the answering machine could pick up. The payphone spit out his quarters. He slotted them back in and dialed again.

This time she answered even before the first ring had finished sounding. "Hello?" she said, breathless, her voice high.

He didn't say anything. For a long moment he simply listened.

"Hello?" she said again, and now he heard the suspicion beginning to cloud her voice.

"It's me," he offered. "Drago."

For a long moment there was silence. He thought she might have hung up. "You've got some fucking nerve," she said.

"Look," he said.

"Give her back!" she said. "Bring her home right now."

"You don't have her?" he asked.

"What?" she said, startled.

"Dani," he said. "You didn't take her?"

She started to say something, then stopped. She started again, then released a high, keening wail. "What kind of sick game are you playing with me now? What have you done with my daughter?"

"I haven't done anything with her," he said. She didn't say anything. He stayed listening for a long time. "Margaret?" he finally said. "I'm not toying with you. I can't find her. I can't find Dani. Do you have any idea where she could be?"

"You bastard," she hissed. "I've recorded this and had the call traced. If anything's happened to—"

Quickly, he hung up. So, she didn't have Dani. At least there was that. As for the call, let her trace it. It wouldn't tell her much: only the city where he lived. And how was she even to know he had called from a city he actually lived in? No, he was still safe.

But what about Dani? Was Dani safe?

It had not been his fault, he told himself. Sometimes things just happen and you can't do anything about them. Just as with the scar on Dani's temple—that had not been, when you considered it logically, his fault. It had simply been bad luck. He could see that even if his ex-wife never would. If she had been able to listen to his point of view, really listen, take a clearer view of things, then they would never have split up. If they'd never split up, she would never have gotten the judge to agree to him only having monitored visitation. He would not have had to make the choice he had made, one day, during one of those visitations. The state-appointed monitor was texting on her phone while he tried to have a meaningful connection with his daughter in the eating room of a children's museum— not even a café, since no food was for sale, simply a room where you could eat your own food if you happened to have remembered to bring food, which he fucking hadn't. How was he to know there was no café? Dani was hungry and crying and the state-appointed monitor was apologizing but saying she couldn't allow them to go somewhere else to get food, because the agreement meant that Dani had to stay there. Of course Drago could go get food, and probably should, the monitor said, but Dani would have to remain with her. And, she emphasized, it would come out of his visitation time. If his wife had listened to his point of view, he would never have— after taking Dani to what she called the potty, instead of returning to the court-appointed monitor—walked right past her holding Dani in his arms as she, the monitor, continued to text. Even then, his only plan had been to take Dani across the street for a bite to eat. Easier to get forgiveness than ask permission and all that. But before he knew it, he had Dani in the back seat—he didn't have a car seat, true enough, his bad, so he made a cushion for her with his jacket and that was enough—and was driving, stopping only long enough to take all the money out of his bank account before leaving town with his daughter forever. But if you kept in mind all the steps, thought very carefully about what had led to what, it was hard not to conclude, as Drago had concluded, that it was not his fault the way everything had all happened, but the fault of his ex-wife.

He hadn't thought about all that in a while. The last six months had been about *not* thinking about that. They had been about establishing a meaningful relationship with his daughter. At first, Dani had been resistant, had kept asking for her mother. But once he told her that her mother was dead and that all she had left in the world was him, she had started to get over it. They had lived in the car for a few days, a week maybe, then he'd found a house to rent in the rougher part of a city, somewhere they could live until their money ran out. First thing he'd done was put in dead bolts. He kept both keys around his neck—not to keep Dani a prisoner so much as just to keep her safe. Then he'd nailed the windows shut, driving the nails in at an angle so that they couldn't be picked out easily. It had only taken her one punitive trip down to the basement to understand and accept that she wasn't allowed to leave the house—he was proud she was such a quick learner: she was more like him than her mother in that way.

After a year, he figured, everything would be o.k. After a year, Dani would love and trust him and he could take a job and enroll her in school. Maybe they would even reach a point where he could start calling himself Drago Borozan again, not Tom fucking Smith. And maybe by that time Dani's mother would have accepted how much she had had a role in everything that had gone wrong and they could have a serious talk and both of them could work out a new custody arrangement that would give them equal parenting time with their little girl.

They could have gotten there if Dani hadn't vanished. With Dani gone, though, he couldn't see a way back to that other life.

He was exhausted when he finally got home. It was quite late, almost midnight. He searched the house once again. She still wasn't there. When he looked out the window of his room, he could see the emaciated woman from next door at her own window, watching him. He closed the blinds.

What had that woman said? She had seen someone who might have been him, but had never seen his daughter? Strange. It was almost as if she didn't believe he'd ever had his daughter there with him.

He opened a can of soup, heated it, drank it down. It made him feel warm, comfortable, which in turn made him feel guilty. He sat on the couch for a little bit. Eventually he climbed the stairs and went to bed.

He was lying there, half-awake, almost drifting off, when he heard it again. The off-key stifled singing coming through the wall. Once he heard it, he realized he'd been hearing it for some time.

He left the bed and crept to the wall, pressing his ear against it. Yes, there was something, a singing, and it sounded like his daughter's voice, like Dani's voice. There were words, he thought, although he couldn't make them out. He wasn't, come to think of it, absolutely sure they were words, and yet there were pauses and shifts that felt like a language of sorts.

He pulled his head away from the wall. Slowly, he moved toward the door. He opened it as quietly as possible, wincing as it creaked. Maybe she would be there, he told himself; maybe she would be waiting for him. Maybe everything would go back to normal: back to just her and him.

But by the time he threw open the door to her room the sound had stopped. He turned on the light. The room looked exactly as he had left it: the bed pulled a little way away from the wall, the circle of objects around it. His daughter was nowhere to be seen.

What does it mean to be me? he wondered, later that night. He was not in his own bed but his daughter's. After not finding her, he hadn't been able to bring himself to leave the room. He had carefully broken the circle, moving aside his daughter's coat, her teddy bear, and then stepped inside and closed the circle again. The bed was too small for him, and his feet hung off the end. He lay there, trying to feel some sign of his daughter's presence. All he could feel was his own ungainly self.

What does it mean to be me? He had lived, it seemed to him, several lives, and when he strung them together they didn't seem to make any kind of chain. Whatever continuity was supposed to be there seemed to have dissolved and he didn't know how to get it back. Even in just the last two years, there had been a life where he and his wife had been together and had been happy, followed by a life where he had been alone and miserable, followed by a life with just him and his daughter, followed by this life now, the one that was now beginning. What did it all add up to? Nothing. Merely four separate existences. He wasn't the same person in any of them. Or rather, in the first three he was three different people. For this life, the newest one, it was still too early to say what, if anything, he was.

At some point, he was not sure when, he fell asleep. He dreamed that he awoke in the same room, with everything exactly the same as it really was. He was in his daughter's bed, still groggy, and he could see there, on the other side of the makeshift circle, his daughter, standing still, attentive, watching him. When he got out of bed and moved toward her, he found he could not cross the border of the circle. *As if I'm a demon,* he thought. He prowled along inside the circle, edging around the bed, looking for a way out. But there was no way out.

For a long time his daughter watched him. He tried to speak to her but no sound came out. As for her, she did not speak at all. She just watched him, as if expecting something, and when she didn't get whatever it was she wanted she turned and walked out of the room.

He could no longer see her, although he could still hear her. He heard her descend the stairs. He followed her footsteps down, one after another, until, from one footstep to the next, the sound ceased.

And then he heard the crash of the door breaking in, shouting, saw a great flash, smoke. Men were yelling and screaming at him to put his hands up and not move and waving guns in his face and he was being forced to his knees and out of the circle, which, somehow, now he could cross.

Many things happened after that, all of them too quickly for his taste. Two detectives took him to a small room and questioned him, asked him where his daughter was, what he had done with her. All he could say was he didn't know. He didn't know. Yes, he had taken her, abducted her if they wanted to insist on that term, but then she had disappeared, he didn't know where she was. Had he killed her? Of course not, he loved his daughter, loved her dearly: he could never have killed her. How could they think such a thing?

"You abducted your daughter a few months after striking her hard enough to fracture her skull and leave her with a scar. How could we think anything else?"

The light was too bright. He couldn't see who had said this exactly—one of the detectives no doubt, although the voice didn't sound like either of their voices. He tried to explain that even though, yes, he'd lost her, she had suddenly reappeared again, only moments before they'd arrived. That he had woken up and seen her, and then she had left the room. And then they'd rushed in. How was it possible they hadn't seen her on their way in?

A trial of sorts, a conviction. He muddled through from one day to the next. His ex-wife came to see him in jail and sat on one side of a plexiglass wall, and they spoke to one another through telephone receivers.

"Where is she?" was the first thing his ex-wife said.

"I don't know," he said. "You have to believe me."

"Please," his ex-wife said, "please. For my sake. Even if you killed her, Drago, tell me. I need to know."

But he simply shook his head helplessly. Soon she was telling him she was glad he was in jail, that he was a horrible person. His arrest, she taunted, had been his own doing. Didn't he know they no longer needed time to trace a phone call? That as soon as he'd called from the payphone they'd known where he was? And was he an idiot, not knowing that the bus station lot had cameras? They had his license plate right away, even knew what direction he'd left in. Even then, it would have taken a few days for them to comb the streets before they spotted his car. But a neighbor of his had called, an elderly woman, and reported that her neighbor was acting strange, claiming he had lost his daughter when there'd never been a daughter so far as she could tell in the first place. Two officers went to investigate and there was his car. Fifteen minutes later, the SWAT team was there. How could he have been so careless?

"Because I was looking for my daughter," he said evenly. "That was all I cared about."

"Just tell me," she said, her voice rising. "Tell me what you did with her!" And soon she was screaming and clawing at the plexiglass, and they were dragging her away.

And then he woke up. He was fully awake this time, and knew that he was, that this time it was real. There was no daughter in the room: there was nobody in the house but him. But which him was it?

He got out of bed and approached the edge of the circle. At his feet a pair of small socks, a postcard, a salvaged doll missing an arm. Still remembering his dream, he expected it to be difficult to cross the barrier. It was like crossing over nothing. If he was a demon, he must be a very powerful one. Before he knew it, he was on the other side. Other than that, nothing had changed. He was still alone, no daughter.

He went back to his own room. It was morning, early still. He put on the T-shirt and jeans he'd been wearing the day before, then sat on the edge of his bed and laced up his shoes. He wasn't sure what to do with himself, where to look next.

Downstairs, he started heating water for coffee. While he stood at the stove, he caught movement out the window.

Two police officers were at the neighbor's house. She was out on the porch in her bathrobe despite the cold, her oxygen tank beside her, glaring into the morning sun. Breath was coming out of her in clouds. He imagined the chirping of her cannula.

She pointed at his house. The policemen turned to look too.

He backed away from the window, still observing them best he could. Slowly they made their way over. He moved from window to window, following their progress. They were walking casually, as if what they were doing was no big deal. They passed his car and were almost to the front door when one grabbed the arm of the other and pulled him back. They both stared at the car, the license plate, talking. One spoke into his radio, quietly. After a moment, the low crackle of a reply. Then they both were moving, more determined now, back to their police car. They got in and waited.

The water was boiling. He turned off the stove, poured the water into the cup, spooned some instant coffee into it, stirred. The jangle of the spoon against the cup was like faraway music. If he stirred exactly right, he could imagine he was catching just the hint of his daughter singing softly, at some distance away.

He would stir the coffee a little, take a sip, maybe two. Soon, he knew, things would come to a head. Another three minutes, maybe four. He would still have time to decide if, when they broke down the door, he would do as they instructed and raise his hands in the air and get down on the ground or if he would ignore his dream and do exactly the opposite, reach as if for a weapon and let them kill him. Did he even want to live in a world like this, one that was always threatening to come unraveled around him?

Either way, he knew he would never see his daughter again. He would never know what had become of her or what, if anything, he'd had to do with it. He took a sip of coffee. If you looked at it right, he tried to tell himself then, even if he had killed his daughter, it was hard to see that it was his fault. After all, how could it be his fault if he couldn't even remember? Was he, now, even the same person? Probably even a lie detector would declare him innocent.

He took another sip of coffee and moved closer to the front door. He was ready. He thrust one hand deep into his pocket. *Sing them in, Dani,* he thought. *Darling daughter, let them come.*

The Second Door

1.

After a while—we had by then lost track of not only the day but also what month exactly it was—I realized that my sister had begun to speak in a language I could not understand. I cannot mark a moment when this change occurred. There must have been a period when she'd spoken it, or some mélange of English and this new tongue, and I, somehow, didn't notice, responding instead to her gestures or to what I thought she must have been saying. But then something, some sound, a clatter of metal falling, caught my attention and I looked for the tin or the pan that had been dropped and realized the sound was proceeding from her mouth.

Was it me? I wondered at first. Some slippage in my brain, some malfunction of my hearing apparatus? I shook my head to awaken my mind, scraped the inside of each earhole with my smallest fingers.

"Come again?" I said.

Her brow furrowed. She spoke again, that same clatter of metal, incomprehensible. It was not the sort of sound that was possible for a human throat to make, and yet her throat made it.

...

But I am getting ahead of myself. I have lived alone now for long enough to no longer have a proper sense of how to convey a story to another being. Even before I lived alone, it was only my sister and me, and our relationship was, shall we say, peculiar. Even before she lost her ability to speak in the way humans do, she was odd, and we had lived together so long as to make the need to converse with one another nearly superfluous. We did speak, occasionally, but gestured more often than moved our lips, and in general lived in that brusque and silent accord enjoyed, if *enjoyed* is the right word, by certain long-married couples. Or so my sister suggested to me. Besides us, I have not met any couples, long-married or otherwise, so I cannot say with certainty.

Not that we were living as if married—no, our relations were at all times innocent and chaste, as if we were merely those children's dolls that give every appearance of being human until you remove their clothing and see the smooth plane where genitalia would otherwise be. Still, we had been so long in one another's company that she knew nearly always what I was thinking and I knew the same about her. We shared that odd intimacy that comes from living partly in one's own head and partly in another's.

I loved my sister deeply, or as deeply as any sexless doll could. Perhaps I have exhausted that metaphor. I do not wish to suggest I am, or ever have been, anything other than human. I was born in the usual way, the issue of a mother and a father—so I have been told. I have no memory of my parents, though my sister always insisted that yes, we had a mother and a father. It is important to note this fact, though I cannot independently verify it. By the time my memories began, my parents were dead.

My sister would sometimes recount their deaths to me late at night, as she was trying to coax me to sleep, acting this out with the two poseable dolls that we possessed. To comfort me, I suppose. An odd notion of comfort, indeed, and yet hearing stories about their deaths allowed them to be alive again for me for just a moment, before they were once again consigned to death. She told the story each time in a different way so that I was never quite sure what the truth was. Indeed, I half suspected that one evening she would not recount their deaths at all, that she would confess that my parents were still alive and waiting for me somewhere—in a concealed room in the house, say, or through the door set in one side of the house that we never used. But whether she intended to tell me this or not, she did not do so before her speech changed and she could tell me nothing at all.

In many of the versions she told of the story, my parents were settlers, pioneers, the first in this place, and because of a failure of some kind, left alone, just the two of them. Sometimes she said we were in a remote area of a southern continent and my parents had been the only survivors of a boat that sunk. Sometimes it was a separate world entirely and they had arrived through the air or by slipping underneath the usual order of things or by passing through a mirror.

"Separate world," I mused. "Separate from what?"

"From where they came from," my sister said.

"And where was that?" I asked.

But she shook her head. For her, this was not part of the story.

There they were, the two dolls that represented my parents, my sister's hands making them jump up and down slightly as she moved them across my blanket. She made my father speak in a voice that was lower than hers, my mother higher. They stopped, looked around.

"Do you suppose it's safe?" asked my mother in her high voice. "Should we turn back?"

"We can't turn back," my father said. "We have no choice."

And then they were screaming, moved by sleight of hand under my blanket, made to vanish, simply gone.

"Again," I said. Smiling, my sister obliged.

...

Whatever the case, whatever had happened to my parents, it had something to do with our house, which was not, as my sister informed me, properly speaking, a house. Its windows were circular and made of thick glass and could not be opened without removing a series of screws and prying off a rubberized seal and a sturdy metal ring. There were two dozen of these windows, strung down a long cylindrical central hallway that constituted the majority of our dwelling. At one end, traveling gently downslope, was a hatch that led to my room. The room had the same circumference as the cylindrical hallway but a depth of no more than seven or eight feet. At the other end of the hallway, upslope, was a hatch leading to the room that had become my sister's, a kind of tapered cone with glass walls that had been burnt a smoky and opaque black.

In the middle of the central hallway, on each side, was a door, a window in its upper half. One side looked out on what seemed to be a flat and barren plain—as did all the windows in the hallway not on a door. The other door's window opened onto deep darkness, as if onto nothing at all.

The first door, to the plain, could be used in time of need, my sister taught me. The second door, no, never. To open the second door would be to invite the end.

"What do you mean by 'the end'?" I asked.

Again, she just shook her head.

"What's out there?" I asked, peering through the window of the second door, through the only window that looked out into darkness. "Is anything out there?"

"Don't open that door," she said firmly. "Promise me."

Despite my promise, I tried once to open the second door. There was a procedure required for this to happen, a process inscribed on the door itself. First the door had to be primed, and then a countdown would begin. Finally, I would have to throw a lever and the door would spring open.

I got as far as priming the door. I had not realized that this would also trigger a dimming of the lights and the peal of an alarm. The sound brought my sister running from her room, her face creased with panic. She quickly unprimed the door and scolded me. The whole time she was doing so, I was wondering if I had the strength of will to disable her and continue the process.

Apparently, I did not.

When my sister was still alive, we kept mainly to ourselves, to our own quarters. My sister referred to them as *quarters* and so I did as well. We would meet for meals in her *quarters,* feeding off the provisions that were stored behind the panels of the central hallway.

Eventually, my sister never tired of informing me, our provisions would run out. In preparation for this, she had begun to forage outside. Sometimes she would slip through the door—the first door, not the second—and come back with something to eat. She would be gone mere minutes sometimes, other times hours. Often, when I was young especially, I would stand by the door and await her return. Sometimes I would go instead to the second door and consider pursuing the procedure to open it, but I worried that my sister, who, after all, knew my thoughts almost as well as I did, was waiting for this, just outside the first door, and would stop me if I tried.

I often at these moments placed my hand on this second door. It was cold to the touch. It would have taken a mere flick of the wrist to activate the sequence, and yet I never did.

When she returned, she was dragging a carcass of a sort of creature unlike anything she had taught me about: a tangle of legs, oozing clusters of eyes, limbs that continued to throb even in death. Or simply gobbets of flesh, still weeping blood, cut from what creature I couldn't say. Out of breath, she would drag her latest find into her quarters and close the hatch. When she next opened it, there would be no sign it had ever been there.

"What's out there?" the dolls that were my parents would sometimes say as they were propelled across my blanket by my sister's hand.

"Why does the view out the first door's window look so different from the view out of the second? Why is there darkness beyond only one door?"

But they never had an answer.

"Shall we go through the first door?" one would say to the other.

"Shall we go through the second?" the other might respond.

If the dolls went out the second door, they would die immediately. If they went out the first door, they might wander for a time before eventually dying.

"Either way, they die," I pointed out.

"Yes," said my sister. "Remember that. In the end, they always die."

Why did the view from that door's window look so different from the other windows?

I asked my sister this, expecting her, like the dolls of our parents, whom she in fact spoke for, to have no answer. I was surprised when she gave the question serious consideration.

"It is as though we are in two places at once," she finally said. "One door opens onto one place, and the other on to another."

"Then," I said, steadying myself on the wall beside me, "what place does that make this?"

"No place," she said. "This is not a place at all."

But if something is not a place, what is it? Can it be said to be anything? And what can be said of those living within it?

2.

My sister had always been the one to instruct me. In the absence of my parents, she fed me, clothed me, reared me. Everything I know about what it means to be human I know from things she said to me or from images, moving or still, she showed me on the still-functioning screen in her quarters. Now that she is gone, the screen will not work for me. I wonder sometimes how much of what I think I know is embroidered falsely upon these images, is my mind working with what it was given to create another, fuller, more promising world.

"Can you understand me?" I asked her.

She nodded.

"Say yes," I said.

A distressed screech, proceeding unnaturally from her mouth, though she did not seem unsettled by it. Indeed, she seemed placid, calm.

"Do you not hear that?" I asked. "How you sound?"

A long hesitation, then she shook her head. She opened her mouth and it was suddenly as if I were inside a car as it crashed, metal buckling and crumpling all around me.

I fled.

Another attempt, an hour later, perhaps two, once I had steeled myself again. There I was, knocking on her hatch until she opened it.

"Hello," I said.

When she responded, in a low whisper, it was as if a pot was being scoured by sand. I winced, and she immediately fell silent.

I extended to her a writing pad, a pen. "Perhaps this will work better," I said.

She nodded and took them with a little bow. Furiously she scribbled on the pad, filling first one page, then a second. When she finally, triumphantly, handed the pad back to me, however, it was covered only in senseless script, clotted and gnarled: gibberish.

For a time, we simply avoided one another. I hoped from one day to the next that something would change, that I would simply awaken one morning and find everything to have reverted back to normal, to have us both speaking the same language again. Instead, with each day, the gap between us grew until, after a week, a few weeks, once the plain outside the first door glittered with frost, it was as though there had never been intimacy between the two of us at all.

The meals we had shared before we now took separately, each in our own quarters. If I came out of my quarters to find her in the central hall, I would turn around and retreat, and if the situation were reversed she would do the same.

We might have gone on like this a very long time, until the day I discovered her body lying facedown in the hall or she discovered mine. Instead, something happened.

My sister would still, despite everything, sometimes leave in search of food. She would go out the first door and be gone an hour, a day. She returned burdened by hunks of bluish flesh or hauling the gooey remains of a carapace.

When I heard her leave the house, as soon as I was sure I was alone, I went out into the hallway and stood by the door, the second door, and pondered opening it. I would stand with my hand on the mechanism, staring out the window into the darkness, staring at nothing, until I heard the sound of the first door opening and my sister returning. Then I would rush back to my quarters.

Until one day, staring into the darkness, staring at nothing, I realized that there was something there after all.

How long I had been staring, I didn't know. Long enough to feel as if I were no longer in my body, as if I were nowhere at all. And then something, a flicker or flash of movement in the glass, caught my attention and brought me back.

It was, I thought at first, a reflection of my face, the ghost of my own image caught in the glass and cast back at me. As I moved my own face slightly, smiled, inclined my head, the ghostly image in the glass reacted precisely as expected. It was only when I settled again, stared out again, motionless, that I realized the flicker was still there.

I held very still. It was there, deep in the darkness beyond the glass, drawn perhaps to this face (my own) it saw through the glass. I waited. I watched and waited.

And yes, there it was, features nearly aligned with my own reflection. There was barely anything there, and yet there *was* something there.

By the time my sister returned, I was back in my quarters, turning over what I had seen. A face, almost like my own but not quite, nearly submerged in the murk. I had the dolls—my sister had abandoned them in my room and had not retrieved them after her voice transformed—and with these I played out what had happened.

The doll that had been my father I designated to be me. He walked down the long, cylindrical hall, in the trough formed between my legs by the dip of the blanket. Halfway down, at the hall's knee, the doll stopped and looked out the thick circular window set in the door. Did he see anything? No, he did not. Or did he? He wasn't sure, he almost turned away, and then suddenly—

There, pushing up against the blanket from beneath, the other doll, the one who had been my mother. What was it now? The doll that was me couldn't make out her features through the blanket, not clearly, though he knew that something was there, something roughly human in form.

It was only a question of how to coax her out from the darkness.

A number of days passed before my sister went outside again. I waited impatiently, hardly leaving my room, afraid to show too much interest in the second door while my sister was still inside. But then at last, finally, she left.

I rushed immediately to the second door, peering out into the darkness. I waited. Nothing was there. And then, though I could see little more than my own reflection, I felt something was.

"Hello?" I said. "Don't be afraid."

Nothing changed or moved, not a thing.

"Please," I said, "let me see you." But as I said it I realized that I didn't need to see to know. That something, an idea, had already begun to coalesce in my mind.

And just like that, I knew who it was.

3.

When my sister, or rather the being that had taken the place of my sister, returned to the first door, it could not open it. I had locked it from the inside. It pounded on the door, crying out in that language that was not a language. Though I could not understand a word of what it said, or even be sure that what it said were words, I knew what it wanted: to get in. It had killed my sister and taken her shape, her manners, her gestures, her whole being, but something had slipped and it could not take her speech. If I hadn't sensed my true sister, the dead one, floating in the darkness behind the glass, I would never have known.

I let the creature pound. It would not get in. Not again.

It is still there, still pounding, its face crusted with frost. I see it in those brief moments when I tear myself away from the second door. It has been there for days now. I know what it wants—its gestures are clear enough. *Open the door,* they say, *open the door!*

And yes, I have come to believe this is something I should do: open the door. Only not the door it desires me to open.

In my bed, I play with the dolls. My father is no longer my father: he is me. My mother is no longer my mother: she is my sister. Not the pretender: the real one. The male doll goes down the hall and stops to stare through the dark window set in the door. He sees something. Or not sees exactly: senses. He is sure something is there. Or rather *someone.* Impossible, since she is dead, but somehow still there nonetheless. He waits, and watches, and then he initiates the procedure. He arms the door. The countdown begins, lights flash, an alarm sounds. And then, after a moment, he is free to throw the lever and open the door and join his real sister. There she is, billowing out of the darkness, her head torn off, coming toward him.

I record this in a language that I, at least, can understand, having as I do no other. Whether anyone else will come who can understand remains to be seen. Though not by me: I am going to step out onto the dark side of our house that is not a house. I am going to rejoin my sister. The real one. The one who is dead.

I will not be coming back.

Or rather, when I do come back, as soon as I open my mouth to speak, you will know it is not me.

Sisters

We had just moved in, hadn't even done anything to our neighbors yet. We were all alone at the end of the block, and already Millie was complaining. Was this going to be another of those stays where we hardly ever left the house? Couldn't we at least join in celebrating the holidays?

"They're not our holidays," Mother explained. "We're not like them."

Millie just stamped her foot. "I *am* from around here," she said. "I am. Now."

Father rolled his eyes and left the room. I could hear him in the other room, the creak of the liquor cabinet as he opened the door, the glug of his pour. It was a big pour. Tonight we would probably leave him to sleep on the floor.

"No," said Mother. "You're not. At least they wouldn't think so."

Millie turned to me. "I mean, you know what they do?" she asked. She said it as if she were addressing me, although she was really saying it for Mother, so I didn't bother to nod. "It's crazy. One holiday involves brightly wrapped gifts. A laughing man climbs up on the roof and throws them down the chimney. If

51

there's a fire in the fireplace, the gifts burn up in the fire. Doesn't that sound fun?"

Well, yes, to me, it did. To Mother too, I knew, but she shook her head. "Where did you hear about this?" she asked.

"I hear things," Millie said. "I make an effort to stay informed. And another," she said, her gaze inching back toward me, "they take a large candle and they knead it and prod it until it becomes nine candles and then they light them all without touching a flame to them."

"I don't think you have that quite right," murmured Mother.

"And there's another one, where you look at yourself in the mirror and keep looking until you can see through your skin, and then you draw your own heart and send the drawing in a letter to someone else."

"Why would you do that?" I couldn't stop myself from saying.

"So that they can control you," she said. "You are saying, 'I do not want myself and so I am giving you the gift of me.' Or something like that."

"It's very strange here," I said.

"Yes," said Millie. "Very strange. And another one where you dig up a tree in one place and then carry it to a different place and then plant it there. A sort of tree-stealing day."

"It's a tree-planting day," said Mother. "And most of them around here don't even know it's a holiday. Almost nobody celebrates it."

"But you have to get a tree from somewhere," Millie insisted. "If you're going to plant it, don't you have to dig it up from somewhere first? It seems to me that it's more a tree-stealing day than a tree-planting day."

Mother shrugged.

"Can we at least steal a tree?" asked Millie.

"Absolutely not," said Mother.

"Why not?" Millie whined. When Mother didn't answer she sighed and went on.

"And then there's the one where we put on a face not our own and go from one door to the next and take things, and—"

But Mother had reached out and grabbed her arm. "Where did you hear about this?"

"I," said Millie. "The immature specimens down the street, I was listening to them as they walked to the instructional center. They were talking about it."

"Did they see you?"

"No, of course not," said Millie. "I would never—"

"And what did they say this day was called?"

"Halloween," said Millie.

"Hallows' Eve?"

Millie considered, shrugged. "Maybe."

Mother let go of her arm. "Now that," said Mother, "that is something we can celebrate. That's not their holiday: it's ours."

That, for Millie, was permission enough. For the next several weeks Halloween was all she could speak about. Any moment she heard voices outside she was out there stalking them, hidden, listening. She was out there so much that people began to sense her. Not see her, exactly, but they began looking over their shoulders more often, increasingly sure they were missing something.

"Don't get caught, Millie," I warned her, "or you'll end up like Aunt Agnes."

"What happened to Aunt Agnes?" she asked, seemingly innocently. But when she saw my expression, she said, "Joking. Don't worry. I won't get caught."

Millie was outside the house more often than not, gathering facts about the holiday, getting the local take on the thing. Father didn't like it, and retreated more and more often to the liquor cabinet, which, perhaps because he had created it, proved surprisingly endless. Before long, he was spending so much time passed out on the floor that the walls of the house began to run and grow furzed around the edges. Mother had to kick him awake and walk him into semi-sobriety, or else we would have been off to the next place, or maybe to no place at all.

About two weeks in, Millie gathered the family together to report what she had learned. She had been, as it turned out, to an instructional center, and had benefited, from her vantage in the coat closet, from a series of short sermons related to the "true" nature of "Halloween." These included the carving of pumpkins into the shapes of those rejected by both heaven and hell, the donning of costumes (by which she meant a sort of substitute skin affixed over the real skin, though in this locale they used an artificial rather than, as we were prone to do, an actual skin), and the "doorstep challenge." This last one, she said, was accompanied by slapping the face of the respondent with a glove, and then saying something such as: "Shall you accept a trick from my hand, or shall you satisfy the aggression of that same hand by soothing it with a treat?"

"That was how it was phrased?" asked Mother.

Millie shrugged. "No, not exactly. I'm improving it."

"And the glove slap?"

"Also an improvement," she admitted.

But improving it, Mother told us, was not something we were meant to do with the holiday. If we were to practice this holiday, we should do our best to practice it exactly as it was done locally. We needed to fit in.

"Even the artificial skin?" asked Millie.

Mother hesitated. "You have a particular skin in mind?" she asked. "Other than the one you currently wear?"

"Oh yes," said Millie, "very much so."

Mother thought for a while. Then Father slurred from the adjacent room, "Hell, let the girls have their fun." And so she shrugged and acquiesced.

The plan was for me to tie Millie's current skin to a chair and then for her to tie mine to a chair, and then she would lead us to the new artificial skin she had in mind. "You'll like it," she said to me. "Once you've tried this new skin, you won't want to come back."

"But you will come back," Mother warned.

"Of course," said Millie. Though from the way she said it, I knew it would be reluctantly.

The tying down of Millie's current skin went smoothly, particularly since she waited to extrude herself until the skin was firmly restrained. I watched her ooze out through the nostrils and become once again just Millie plain and simple. The skin was for a moment inert, and then it came to itself, beginning to scream, then screaming full throated until Mother gagged it.

"What do you suppose it remembers?" asked Millie, her voice papery and whisper thin beside me, a kind of light flutter against my eardrum. "Does it know how I've made use of it?"

"It must know something," I said. "Otherwise it wouldn't be screaming."

What we hadn't considered was that now, out of her skin, Millie couldn't tie my own skin to a chair. And I could hardly tie myself up. "Shall I go borrow a skin," whispered Millie, "and bring it back to do the job?"

Mother sighed. "I'll handle it," she said.

She tied me tight—she had had the most practice—and also pushed a cloth deep into my mouth while I was still in the skin: easier that way. And then I wriggled about inside the flesh and slowly detached myself and, panting, dragged myself out.

Millie led me, a flitting form. Still panting, I tried to keep up. Mother was there at the door, arms crossed, watching us go. It felt good to be out, good to be able to stretch. *Why even bother with a new skin?* I wondered. But when I voiced this to Millie, she scolded me.

"This is important," she said. "We're getting to know them, seeing how they celebrate. Once we understand that, we'll understand much more, and soon we won't have to move so often and may even start to feel like we're them."

"Why would we want to feel like that?" I asked.

She ignored this. She led me to a telephone pole, one without climbing pegs on the side, and then sped up it. I followed. A moment later we were beside the wire, the buzzing loud, and louder of course because we were there. And then she slipped into the current and flowed away.

I followed. I could barely keep up, and nearly lost track of her in the flow. Too late, I saw her clamber out. I had to force myself back hard against the current and barely managed to reach the stepdown. By the time I pulled myself out, Millie was already across a lawn and headed toward the porch of a house. It wasn't a *true* house, like ours was. You had the sense, even from a single glance, that it was made of nothing but brick and wood and mortar, not likely to last more than a few dozen years, and was rooted stolidly to one spot. What good, really, was a house like that? Why she was interested in it at all was impossible for me to say.

"Look," she said.

And there it was: on the porch, half hidden behind the bushes, a mannequin of some kind, a black tattered dress, face made to look old, long white hair, a dark peaked hat, eyes like burning coals. We approached with care but something about it saw us in a way that the locals had not, and it began cackling at our approach, its eyes strobing.

"What is it?" I asked. "Some kind of moving statue?"

"You can get inside," she said. "Go ahead, climb in."

And so I did. Not climb so much as flow quickly in. It was a different sensation from the fleshy skins I usually occupied, and decidedly stiff. The arms moved just a little, constrained as they were. The head swiveled a few inches in either direction. The legs wouldn't move much at all. A moment later my sister had forced her way in as well.

"Hey," I said. "It's tight in here."

"Stop grumbling," Millie said. "There's plenty of room."

She was right, mainly. But still, it was awkward with both of us operating the artificial skin from the inside. Slowly we got used to it. Working together, we could force the joints of the arms farther.

We could make the fingers snap open and closed. Together, with effort, we could even make the legs creak and move.

"Now what?" I asked.

"Now, we wait," she said.

We stayed there as night got deeper. A person resembling our father who was perhaps a father himself came out of the house that the porch was attached to and peered at us through thick glasses. He went and fiddled with the cord that was attached to our artificial skin, unplugging it from the wall and plugging it back in again.

"What do you suppose he wants?" I whispered.

"Hush," my sister said.

Eventually, seeming to grow frustrated, he unplugged the cord and went back inside. Once she was sure he wasn't coming back out, Millie said, "The skin must have been made to do something that it's not doing now that we're inside."

"It was doing something when we arrived," I said. "Eyes glowing, sounds of some sort. Cackling maybe, or screams."

"Eyes glowing, cackling, screams," said my sister. "I can manage that." And she started rummaging around within the thing until the porch was bathed in a deep red glow and a sound box embedded within the artificial skin was making noises like a giant being strangled.

"Too loud," I shouted. "Too much light!" She let it all go at once, the porch immediately dark and silent.

A moment later the man burst through the door and back onto the porch, looking frantically around. He regarded the unplugged cord a long moment and then, mumbling and shaking his head, went back inside.

"What was that all about?" Millie asked.

"How should I know?" I said.

We settled in. We waited until the lights inside the house went off, and then we waited as the stars whirled lazily above us. We were good at waiting. The night began to fade and still we waited.

"What are we waiting for?" I asked Millie.

"Shhh," she said. "For the right day. For Halloween to start."

The sun rose and it became warm inside the skin. I stretched and tangled with Millie, and then elbowed her until she gave me space. The day slowly crept by. A family came out of the house attached to our porch, first a father like the one we had seen last night, then two immature specimens, then what we guessed to be a mother. The sun rose and passed above us—not directly overhead but clinging more to one half of the sky. Eventually the family, bit by bit, returned. Or some family anyway—I couldn't be exactly sure they were the same ones.

The sun was just beginning to set when I realized there was someone else inside the skin with us, someone of such presence that she was pushing me up against the walls of the skin, making me start to ooze through.

"Hi Mom," I managed.

"I tell you girls that you can celebrate one holiday and you think that gives you permission to stay out all night."

"No," I said, "I'm just . . . Sorry, Mom."

"Not even a note," she said. "What have I done to deserve this?"

"We weren't doing any harm," said Millie. "We hadn't even gone far."

Mom turned to her. "And you: do you want to end up like Aunt Agnes?" she asked.

"No, Mother," she managed.

For a long time she was silent. I thought she was going to drag us home, that the holiday would be over for us before it even began. And then she sighed. "We'll deal with this tomorrow. Home by midnight," she said, "and straight from here to the wires and then home. No stops!"

"Yes, Mom," I said.

"Millie?"

"Yes, Mom," she said.

"Good," said Mother, and as abruptly as she had arrived, she was gone.

. . .

It was barely dark, the streetlights buzzing on, when they began to come. Small groups of them, two or three, wearing peculiar false skins tightened over their own skins. They were immature specimens, a dozen years along or less. Invariably, they were accompanied by one or two mature local adults who did not wear false skins but instead stood with folded arms at the sidewalk's end, far away from the porch.

"Are they not allowed to come onto the porch unless they are wearing a false skin?" I wondered.

"I don't know," whispered Millie. "If that's the case, why would they come at all if they didn't have one?"

Of the young specimens that came onto the porch, there were those that wore skins resembling animals and those that wore skins resembling the dead. Others chose skins that resembled nothing I had ever seen—strange shining figures with bug-like eyes, figures with veiled faces with symbols emblazoned on their chests. There were even a few that adapted the terrifying species designated *the clown*.

"They don't all take the same sorts of skins?" I asked.

"No," said Millie. "Apparently not. They take skins of all kinds."

"What good is that?" I asked. To this she had no answer.

They stepped onto the porch, walked past us, and approached the door. They rang the doorbell. When the door was open, they cried out the ritual phrase *Trick or treat*. But yet, there was no trick to be had, only the rapid distribution of fistfuls of sweets followed by the shooing of these double-skinned creatures away.

"So, if they don't produce the sweets rapidly enough, that's when the trick comes?" I asked.

"That's my understanding," said Millie. "Then they will soap a window, or throw rotten fruit at a façade, or kill the primary member of the household."

It seemed to me that there was a large gap between the first two tricks she had mentioned and the third. Surely, I suggested, there must be some tricks in between. Such as the severing of a finger, say, or the slow torture of one of the secondary members of the household—an immature specimen, say, or a pet. Even killing someone *other than* the primary member of the household struck me as a viable intermediary step.

But my sister claimed to have her information from a combination of overheard talk and television viewed through the window of the local bar and grill, two sources of authority that, taken in tandem, were difficult to dispute.

Nevertheless, we might have continued to argue had we not both simultaneously become aware that one of the doubly skinned specimens on the porch was regarding not the man with the bowl of sweets at the door, but us.

"Hush," said my sister to me.

But the specimen came closer, then closer still, peering quizzically at the fabric and metal and rubber armature that contained us. The specimen's false skin was colored all orange and black. It sported black boots and an orange skirt. It had a tall black hat, floppy and crimped, impractical in every respect, and carried a black broom. Meant to represent some sort of ancient and inefficient cleaning woman, perhaps.

It came very close indeed, looking right into the eyes of the armature, and then its vision slid down and to one side. I could see that it was looking through the armature and right at my sister.

"What are you doing in there?" it said to her.

In retrospect, I think my sister, so long undetected, so long unseen, was not prepared to be seen. Before I could stop her, she'd taken control of the armature's hands and locked them around the small creature's neck.

There was a commotion on the porch, someone was screaming. The bowl of sweets dropped and shattered and the man who had been holding it was prying at the artificial hand, trying to free the child.

I had a choice. Either I could save the child or I could support my sister. I could add my will to her own and between the two of us we could easily snap the creature's neck. Or else I could loosen her fingers.

In the end I did nothing. Instead, I fled. In just a moment, I was out of the artificial skin and had flowed back down the sidewalk and up the pole and into the wire. A moment later I was back at home, coming conscious within the skin I had occupied before.

Mother was standing there, patiently waiting, wearing her traveling clothes. When she saw I was back, she cut the ropes, quickly freeing me.

"Where's your sister?" she asked.

"She was seen," I said.

She just nodded, her skin's lips a thin line. I got up and massaged my wrists. My father was standing there beside her, an ice pack pressed to his head. "She may still come back," he said.

I sat there, nervously waiting. In the end, yes, she did come, with a deep gasping breath, and in a state of panic. She looked at me with fury.

"You left me," she accused.

I shrugged. "You were seen," I said.

She looked to Mother and Father for support. They remained impassive. She had been seen. She knew the rules. She was lucky we had waited for her at all.

"It can't see me anymore," she said. "No need to worry."

"You blinded it?" asked Father.

"Killed it," she said. "Strangled it." She looked at me again. "No thanks to you," she whispered.

"Don't be snippy," Mother said to her. She belted her coat around her. "Come on," she said, "let's go."

But we had barely thrown open the door when the specimen appeared. It looked exactly as it had before, same orange and black, same unfortunate hat, except for the black marks on its neck. And the fact that, in places, you could see right through it.

"Hello," Mother said.

"Trick or treat," it said.

"Can I help you?" Mother asked. "Are you lost?"

"I . . . don't know," it said.

"Yes," Mother said. "I can help you."

For a long time it was immobile, silent. "Who are you?" it finally offered.

"Me?" asked Mother, bringing her hand to her neck in a way that brought back memories for me. "Why, I'm your mother. Don't you recognize me?"

And that was how our family grew from four to five, and I came to have a new sister. Millie did not seem excited, but I most certainly was. *A new sister,* I thought, imagining all I would be able to teach her, *a new sister!* And teach her I did, and loved her too, for the whole remainder of the evening. Up until the very moment when, as the clock struck midnight and the holiday came to an end, we ate her.

Room Tone

At the last possible moment he found the perfect house. It was empty and spacious and hadn't been updated since the seventies, which was exactly what Filip wanted. It was for sale, with the old couple who had lived there both in hospice now and their children living on the other side of the country and eager to sell. To lease a place like that for a few weeks would normally have cost well over what they had budgeted for locations. But Filip had a word with the Realtor and since they only needed to film at night, she struck a deal with him that involved a lump cash payment of three hundred dollars, a sum that Filip suspected would never make it further than the Realtor's pocket.

"We have a deal," she said. "Remember, at night only. In no earlier than six at night, out by seven in the morning. And for exactly two weeks, starting tomorrow."

He agreed. Of course he did. He figured at the time that the time limit was there so the Realtor would feel like she could ask for more money if they needed a few extra days. Besides, Filip had things under control. He, Filip, was the heart of the project: he had written the thing, he was directing it, he was handling the sound, he was doing the editing in postproduction. He had grown up down the street from the cameraman: they had a rapport, so even though Filip wasn't the cameraman he knew exactly what this particular cameraman would do. The actors, too, were all people he had gone to school with. Which meant that he could see in his head exactly how every piece of the project would go.

But then again, there was the lighting person, who he didn't know, who the producer had brought aboard. He was union, which meant he saw this as a job, complete with overtime. And the producer himself, who he didn't really know, who had come through the cameraman, was a friend of the latter's father. And of course the woman doing wardrobe, the makeup artist, a best boy, a gaffer: they were unknowns too. But, yes, basically, he had his finger on the pulse of the project. He was sure that he could get it done.

On day eleven of the shoot, he went by the Realtor's office. "Done already?" she asked. "No discounts for days not used." But when she realized that Filip was there for precisely the opposite reason, she said, "Let's not talk here."

They walked to a coffee shop around the corner. Over a confused mélange of cider and chai that the coffee shop referred to as *chaider*, Filip explained that there had been unexpected difficulties, that they were running behind. Just a day or two, that was all they needed. He was happy to pay for it.

"No," she said.

"No?"

"As in no," she said. "It can't be done."

He only needed a few days, he told her. He could pay her double the rate he'd paid before. They needed it to finish the movie.

"I'm sorry," she said. "No."

He opened his mouth to speak again, but she had already leaned far back in her chair, her arms folded across her chest, her mouth a tight line.

"Why not?" he asked.

"The house is sold," she said. "I'd sold it before you and I struck our deal. He moves in the day after you finish."

"Isn't there a way of pushing the closing back a day or two?"

She shook her head. "He wanted to move in earlier than that. I've been stalling the escrow just to give you the two weeks I promised. But I can't give you a minute more."

The next three days were difficult. He quickly went back over the script, trimmed any scenes he could justify trimming, regrouped everything to be as efficient as possible. He prayed for single takes. He gathered the actors in a park down the street a few hours before they were allowed to enter the house and rehearsed until they had it just right. It was a struggle, and effort, but in the end, they were almost back on schedule. They might just make it.

But they didn't. The last day, Filip had everyone show up at three rather than six. They had a series of scenes to do in the living room of the house, where the murder took place. The murder scene would have to be shot last of all, because of the fake blood. They couldn't circle back to shoot the earlier scenes once the blood was smeared about, and they'd probably be able to shoot the murder just the once.

But when they arrived at the house, the Realtor was there, showing around a gray-haired, distinguished man. He was, thought Filip, not unlike the man who would be murdered in the script. "—move all this shitty furniture out," he was saying. "I didn't buy this crap. I only bought the house." Then he turned to Filip. "Who are you?" he asked. "What are you doing here?" Behind him, the Realtor was shaking her head no.

"I'm . . . here to make a record of the house," he claimed.

"Record of the house," the man said. "Why?" He turned to the Realtor. "I don't know that I'm comfortable with that."

"It's something the children want," Filip lied. "To be able to remember how the house was when their parents lived there."

"You'll have the house tomorrow," soothed the Realtor. "After that, you can do whatever you want to with it."

"And you'll take the furniture out?" the new owner asked Filip.

"Yes," said Filip. "Absolutely."

The new owner sniffed and then turned away. He wandered with the Realtor to another part of the house. Quickly, they began to set up, though before they had finished the new owner had come back again.

"Are all these lights really necessary?" he asked. "You're recording the contents of the house, not shooting a movie."

"I'm just doing what I've been told to do," said Filip.

"It'll be your house tomorrow," the Realtor said again.

The new owner shook his head and went out.

It was a long night, and even with the extra three hours they quickly fell behind. The Realtor was back an hour later to bawl him out about coming in early. Filip stood and took it. He agreed with her, profusely apologized, did anything he possibly could to satisfy her as quickly as possible so that he could go back to shooting. It was a weird day; everybody seemed a little off. He tried to tell himself that was o.k.— the scenes that were being shot were leading to a murder after all, all the characters were more than a little out of their minds in those scenes, and maybe it was good for the anxiety of the crew to rub off on them. He remembered a performance of a Jean Genet play he'd once seen in Seattle in which the actors kept injuring themselves, tripping, running into things, falling. They did so more and more often as the play went on, so much so that he thought, *If this play goes on for another hour, someone is going to wind up dead.* Maybe it would be like that.

And maybe in the end it was like that, even though they had to close the curtains for the final scene because it was already growing light outside, had to quickly rework all the camera angles so the closed curtains wouldn't be visible. It was like everything leading up to the murder was being shot with a view of the dark sheet of glass that was the front window, but now that the murder was actually going on the room could only be seen from the other side, looking in. That was good—maybe that was good. If it was, then in a way they had the new owner of the house to thank for it. They began filming and yes, the scene came off and the blood went places where they hadn't expected the blood to go, which was, Filip guessed, good. Could be made to look good anyway.

They were almost finished, the scene essentially concluded, the body lying on the floor, throat slit, no longer moving, and the killer standing, straightening his now-bloody jacket and walking toward the front door, when someone turned a key in the lock. The actor playing the killer stopped walking, not knowing what to do. Filip urged him forward. The door opened and the chain caught it and he saw, through the opening, the enraged eye of the new owner.

"What the hell?" the man said.

And maybe that was good, Filip thought, maybe they could use that too—with the resemblance of the new owner to the victim it was almost like a man was walking in on his own murder. Filip's mind was already twisting the details, trying to make it all fit his artistic vision.

"Cut," he said.

"You're still here?" the new owner said, moving his head back and forth across the crack in the door, as if unable to decide whether to look at Filip with his right or left eye. "And the furniture's still here? What's that all over the floor?"

"We're almost done," said Filip. "We just—"

"This is my house," the man yelled, his face going a deep red. "Get out of my house!"

"We need five more minutes," said Filip. "If you can give us that, it will be enough. You'll never have to see us again."

But the new owner already had his cell phone out. The new owner was already dialing.

The police were sympathetic, they really were. Filip explained as much as he could without getting the Realtor in trouble, and the

police were inclined to believe him that it had all been a misunderstanding and to let it go. They made no gestures toward trying to
take his footage. Would he be willing to pay the cost of cleaning
and of moving the furniture out? Of course he would, Filip said. In
fact, he would go in there and personally clean it himself—

But the officer was shaking his head. "No," he said. "Mr. Mason
doesn't want you on the property. He's asked for a restraining order."

But if he were to personally supervise the job then it would be
sure to—

The officer clapped a heavy hand on his shoulder. "He'll send you
the bill. You'll pay it." And, not knowing what else to do, Filip agreed.

2.

It might have ended there, with Filip's producer in slightly over his
head because of Mr. Mason employing not merely a cleaner to take
care of the mess but a forensic cleaner at that, despite it having been
a simulated rather than actual murder. Looking over the footage he
became convinced that yes, they did have enough, they'd be o.k.
Even at the end of the murder scene they'd gotten enough footage before the actor hesitated because of the noise at the door as
Mr. Mason tried to come in. It was obvious he was walking toward
the door; that should be enough, more than enough. They'd simply
jump to him outside the house, slowly pushing his way deep into his
hiding place in the hedge. Viewers would be able to follow it.

So, it was o.k. Or at least he thought it was, until he started
editing the sound. It was mostly fine, but in all the chaos of that last
day, in the jerky start and the awkward final moments, he hadn't
managed to do the very simple thing of recording the room tone.

That was o.k., he told himself. It didn't matter. They could take
a moment in one of the scenes, one of the dead, silent moments,
and simply replicate it until they had a minute, say, of room tone.
But he tried that and it sounded . . . wrong. Not to the producer—
the man couldn't tell the difference—but to Filip. He went back
through the tape, but no, there was no good sustained silence. Or

rather, there was sustained silence, but it was all from moments when the curtains were open and they didn't mesh with that more muffled feeling of having the curtains closed while the murder was happening. That stifled feeling, felt in the audio of the rest of the scene, was something he was missing in the silence.

He told himself it was no big deal, that the movie would be fine without it. But the more time he spent editing, the more he realized this was wrong. He needed the room tone.

When the new owner opened the door, he tried to explain. Yes, he'd been in the house longer than he'd meant to and he wanted to apologize for that. Yes, they'd left a mess and yes, they hadn't been completely honest with him. He was, he claimed, truly sorry for that. When the new owner started to close the door, he managed to wedge his foot into the crack. They always did that in the movies and it seemed to work just fine there, though in real life—maybe because he was wearing sneakers, maybe because the new owner closed the door very hard indeed—it hurt the hell out of his foot.

"I'd just like five minutes," Filip said. "That's all I need." Filip brandished the boom mic. "After that, I'll never bother you again."

"No," said the man.

"But you don't understand, without it the movie—"

"I don't care," said the new owner.

"I'm willing to pay," said Filip.

"I don't want your money," said the new owner. "I want you to get your foot out of my door and get the hell off my porch." And when Filip still persisted: "I have a restraining order against you. If you're not off the porch in twenty seconds, I'm calling the police."

Why twenty seconds? Filip wondered, absurdly, as he left the porch. Why twenty? What was significant about that length of time to the man? If the man would let him in and simply stay quiet for twenty seconds, would that be enough? Well, maybe not. Still, it would be a lot better than what he currently had.

...

"Don't worry," his producer said. "It's not noticeable." Everybody on the crew said the same, no matter how many times he asked them. He suspected they said it because the producer had told them to. The producer was ready to be done with the project. The producer was ready to move on to his next project, his next tax break.

But Filip found himself unable to sleep at night, thinking about the room tone, thinking about the several moments in the movie where you heard the wrong silence. He had to figure something out. He had to do something.

Which is why, a few days later, he was in a car parked down the street, watching the house, waiting for the new owner to leave. The new owner lived alone, it seemed, and so as the afternoon wore on, Filip began to feel that all he had to do was wait until the man went out, and then break in, record for a few minutes, and then leave.

It was early evening before Mr. Mason left. He went out the front door and locked it behind him, then got in his car and drove away. Filip waited a few minutes, just to make sure he wouldn't come back for something, and then he got out of the car and moved toward the door.

He had a rock. He had brought a rock with him. He was wearing gloves too, just in case. He went around back to one of the windows there and broke it with the rock.

Immediately an alarm went off, loud and blaring. *Motherfucker,* he thought. He was already halfway inside, envisioning where he'd stand to record the room tone, how he'd get away before the cops arrived, before realizing that with the alarm blaring there was no way he could record anything at all.

He'd have to go in while Mr. Mason was there. That was the only solution. Surely the man wouldn't set the alarm when he was in the house, sleeping? He'd simply sneak in, late at night, surreptitiously record the room tone, then sneak out again. Mr. Mason would never know he'd been there.

He waited a week, then two. No point going in too soon after the break-in. No, let the man relax a little, let him let down his guard.

He parked down the street, cased the house through a pair of binoculars that he quickly lowered any time a car drove by. By eleven o'clock, Mr. Mason was upstairs in his bedroom, the lights off, the room lit only by the sickly glow of a television. He'd probably be able to sneak in while Mr. Mason had the television on, except the television sound would be picked up by the mic. No, better to wait until late, very late indeed.

At four in the morning, he left his car and ran nimbly to the house. The front door was locked, of course it was, but the window next to it was open just a crack, for the cool air. Which meant the alarm would have to be off, at least the one on that window. A wooden rod kept the window from opening too far, but he could wriggle his hand and most of his arm through. He tore a small branch off the tree near the front walk and then reached in with it and used that to push and prod the wooden rod out of its channel until it fell clattering to the floor.

He waited, listened. No noise, nothing. Mr. Mason hadn't heard.

He slid the window all the way open, popped out the screen. Carefully, he lifted the recording equipment in, then shimmied in himself.

In the dark, he pulled the window shut and closed the drapes. By the glow of a penlight he moved a few of the pieces of furniture around, trying to position them as closely as possible to where the previous furniture had been. He placed the headphones on his head. He positioned the mic and began to record.

The lights flicked on. He spun and there was Mr. Mason, standing on the stairs in a pair of striped pajamas, his face clenched in anger. "What the hell are you doing?" he shouted.

Filip held his finger to his lips. But Mr. Mason wasn't listening. He was coming down the stairs, shouting and gesticulating, spittle flying off his lips, very red in the face.

"You have to be quiet," said Filip.

"I don't have to do anything!" said Mr. Mason. "This is my house. Get out!"

All Filip needed was a minute, maybe two, of silence. Give him that and the movie would be done. But Mr. Mason didn't understand that. Mr. Mason was refusing to understand that.

Filip swung around toward him and the mic boom swung with him. Mr. Mason covered his head and flinched, as if he were about to be struck. Which was when, Filip tried to explain to himself later, he had gotten the idea of hitting Mr. Mason. In a way, he told himself, Mr. Mason himself had given him the idea.

He struck him once in the face, then again. The man went down in a heap, writhing. Filip kicked him in the temple once, hard, and he fell still. *Now,* thought Filip, *now I can record in peace.*

But halfway through, Mr. Mason began to groan.

So, for the sake of art, Filip tied him up. And gagged him. There he was on the floor, struggling, still managing, somehow, despite everything, to make noise, to ruin things.

Sighing, Filip took off the headphones. He knelt down beside Mr. Mason and very calmly explained to him that all he had to do was be quiet for two minutes and then he would untie him and let him get back to his life.

And to be fair to Mr. Mason, he was silent; he did manage to hold still. This time, the recording went smoothly. Filip finally had what he needed.

"There," he said, when he was done. "That wasn't so hard, was it?" And he took off Mr. Mason's gag.

"You fucker," said Mr. Mason. "You shit! You'll go to jail for this. I'll make sure you rot!"

Filip had already reconciled himself to this. There would be a price for finishing his film: he had accepted this. Mr. Mason could not frighten him. Filip had gotten what he wanted and he was willing to pay for it. So he let Mr. Mason blather on while he imagined himself leaving the man tied up as he made his way back to the postproduction studio and inserted silence where silence was needed. He would finish his movie, then he would go to the police and turn himself in and arrange for Mr. Mason to be untied.

It might have worked that way, too, if Mr. Mason hadn't been a fool. Filip, considering the matter in retrospect, when he had a lot of time to think, felt he should have known the fellow was a fool and should have planned accordingly, should have braced himself. But as it was, when Mr. Mason began to threaten not only him but also his movie, he was caught off guard.

"I'll make sure your fucking piece of shit movie never sees the light of day," was the first thing he said. And then Mr. Mason went on to explain, in excruciating detail, how he would manage this.

Perhaps it was the room, the scene he had filmed there some months before and what it suggested to him. Perhaps it was more the thought of something that he'd spent the last five years of his life working on being destroyed. Or perhaps it was simply that he felt Mr. Mason was more irritating than any human should be allowed to be. Whatever the case, a few minutes after the gag was removed, Mr. Mason was dead, his throat cut from ear to ear, the blood spraying everywhere.

He began to move around the house, wiping doorknobs, removing his shoes and smearing the bloody shoeprints into unrecognizability. He changed into a set of Mr. Mason's clothing and burned his own clothing on what he had to admit was a rather nice new Viking stove that Mr. Mason had had installed. He obliterated whatever trace he could that he had been there.

All the while he was doing it, he found something nagging at him, but he wasn't sure what. Only when he was close to leaving and was cleaning the blood off the boom mic in the kitchen did he realize what it was.

He went back into the room, held himself still. Little had changed, and yet with Mr. Mason dead the tone of the room was subtly different. He could hear it. Maybe he was the only one who could hear it, but he could. It was, he was almost certain, better.

And so, standing there in his bloody socks, he turned on the recorder. It would be the thing that made the movie, he felt. The awful weight of that silence, the way it smelled of blood. It would be not only good enough but perfect, and only he would know why it was so.

He stood there, perfectly still, holding the mic. Even after the reel had run out, he remained there, motionless, listening.

Shirts and Skins

On their first date, a so-called blind one, Megan took Gregory by the hand and he let her. She led him into a space afflicted with mood lighting and for a moment he thought it must be a bar, a remarkably empty one, but no, it was not a bar but an art gallery. Or, rather, the cloakroom of a gallery, with a row of hooks on the left wall of the narrow room. On those hooks were a series of what he thought were sweaters but which, as his eyes adjusted, he realized were shirts. So, maybe not a cloakroom after all. She was tugging at his hand, pulling him forward, and then he was there, glimpsing beside the row of hanging shirts a small, unobtrusive card glued to the wall. He bent down, squinted. *Shirts,* read the card.

But she was already heading through the doorway and what, blind date or no, could he do but follow? So he followed, out of that room and into the next. The same narrow room, the same series of hooks, nothing hanging from them this time. And there, just there, just beyond, another unobtrusive card. *No Shirts,* it read.

Correct, he thought, ludicrously.

There she went, heels clopping. Why had she worn heels? It was a blind date but they had agreed to a casual date, during daylight hours. Didn't casual preclude heels? Was she the kind of girl who would wear heels on a casual date or was she on a different sort of date than he was?

He followed. Same room, same row of hooks, a few shirts scattered on them. With dread, he moved toward the small white card. *Some Shirts*, it read.

What the fuck? he wondered.

She had circled back and caught hold of his hand, and now tugged him forward, through a door at the far end of the room, one with a metal bar in the middle of it. She pushed down the metal bar and an alarm went off, screeching, and he stopped, but no, she dragged him through. And then they were out in an alley behind the gallery, blinking in the sunlight. A man was sprawled there, in a mound of trash. He was wearing a coat, zipped closed despite the heat, and a pair of mismatched sneakers, although he had no pants. His flaccid penis curved sleepily to one side. *Shirt or no shirt?* Gregory wondered about him. With the coat, he couldn't tell.

He looked for a white card. He turned to her, confused. "Is this part of the exhibit?" he asked.

He was surprised when Megan became happy, inordinately so. "Right," she said, her face lighting up in a broad smile, "exactly!"

2.

A week later they had moved in together. Gregory couldn't help but feel that their relationship had been established on a misunderstanding. He still couldn't figure out what had happened at the gallery exactly, nor behind it, nor why the sequence as a whole had led to him having what could only be described as profound difficulty asserting his own personality and desires when he was with her. It was as if their relationship, having gotten off on a particular foot, had lopped off the other one—the more independent, healthier foot—and so now he had to hop. Not just the foot, he sometimes thought, but the whole leg. When he was with her, there was less of him and what was there she was somehow in charge of.

She was older than him as it turned out, though she had lied about her age when they had first met, and, indeed, continued to lie about it. But he had glimpsed her proper age, the year anyway, on her driver's license when she had been buying liquor at the grocery store. Her age wasn't, he told himself, a problem in and of itself except to the degree that she felt entitled to control the relationship. For it was she who decided where they would go, what they would have for dinner, how they would spend their day. When they had decided to move in together it had been, in fact, she who had decided they would move in together. And he, even though a part of his mind was screaming the whole time at him to run, had simply gone along with it.

Have I always been like this? he wondered. *Passive?* That, as much as anything, was what worried him. But no, he didn't think so. He'd had relationships in the past. They had, admittedly, all been bad—or at least had all ended badly. But he'd been able to assert himself, to make his will known. For instance, in those other relationships he hadn't, as he now did in this relationship, taken up running because she ran every morning and simply took it for granted he would too. He hadn't been, as he was now, willing to sit for two or even three hours at a stretch watching marathons of a formulaic and unbearable dramedy, about a perky New Yorker who moves to Alabama, on a channel inexplicably called "the cw." The whole time he had felt himself going crazy inside. *What is this relationship doing to me?* he wondered. *What will be left of me once it's done?*

"You're the best," she said during the commercial break, leaning over and stroking his cheek in a way that made him want to flinch. "You're my favorite boyfriend ever." A part of him tried to smile weakly back at her. It hardly mattered; the commercial had ended and her eyes were already glued to the screen.

3.

On their six-month anniversary, over a dinner that she had chosen the recipes for but insisted he make, she brought up the art show again. Now that he'd lived with her as long as he had, he had an even harder time understanding why she'd taken him to it. It didn't fit, at least to his mind, with the other sorts of things she liked. They hadn't gone to a gallery together since.

"Wasn't it wild?" she was saying. "I mean: *Shirts*?"

"Umm," he said.

"And that guy, in the back, his junk all out?"

"I," said Gregory, and straightened. "Was he an actor? Was he part of the show?"

She laughed, in a loud, boisterous way that he had rapidly come to think of as forced. "Right, exactly," she said.

Right? Exactly? What does that even mean? A dull rage began to rise in him. *He seemed liked such a nice, normal guy,* he imagined the neighbors saying. *But then he snapped.* He lifted his wine glass and drained it. When he reached for the bottle, she playfully batted his hand away.

"Slow down, cowboy," she said, and smiled glubbily. It was like being smiled at by a mudskipper.

He was not a cowboy. Why would she call him that? When she got up to *powder her nose,* he poured himself another glass, filled it almost to the brim. By the time she was back at the table, he had managed to drain it.

It was that, probably; the wine. And drinking it so fast. Before he knew it, he was talking, parts of himself coming out that she had until then kept battened in. "I didn't like it," he said.

She snorted. "You cooked it," she said. "It's your own fault."

"No," he said, "not that. The art show."

For just a moment he saw the naked hurt in her face, though it was quickly gone, submerged beneath a more practiced expression.

"You *loved* it," she accused.

"I hated it," he claimed. "I really hated it."

"No, you didn't," she said, her lip curling.

"But I—"

"You've had too much to drink, and now you're saying things you don't mean."

"But—"

"You're being mean," she said. "And on our anniversary too."

He stared at her, confused. No, he knew, he was being honest, much more so than he'd been through the rest of the relationship. Was he? Or maybe she was right—she was always right, in the end. Maybe—

"I want to break up," he managed, while he could still speak his mind.

"No," she said.

"No?"

"You heard me," she said. "No."

"What do you mean?" he asked, voice faltering. "I don't want to? Or that I can't break up with you?"

"Both," she said.

In the morning, he awakened, head throbbing, and stumbled downstairs, where she was already sitting at the table, sipping her coffee. He sat down beside her, ready to be scolded, but she pretended like nothing had happened. Instead, she proceeded to recount a glowing version of their six-month anniversary the night before that bore, he knew, no resemblance to what had actually happened. This scared him much worse than her anger would have. She had already started to shape the event, make it what she wanted it to be, kill what it actually had been.

Just as she had shaped him, and would continue to do so, he knew, until they reached the point where there would be nothing left of him at all.

"Your turn to cook breakfast," she said.

It was always his turn to cook breakfast. And always, he knew, would be.

4.

It was like looking at his life through a smaller and smaller window. Like he was watching it but helpless to control anything. In the end, he couldn't help but think, it would be like she was having a relationship with some version of herself as he tapped his finger on a tiny but thick pane of soundproof glass, calling out silently for help.

He needed friends; friends would help. But he didn't have any. As a couple they had friends, true, but these were really her friends—she hadn't found his suitable. It was as if she had carefully and systematically trimmed away everything that he was connected to except for her.

But why couldn't he be honest with her? Wasn't that his fault? And now it had gone on so long that it was impossible for him to end it. How could he end it? Just say, "Megan, I've been unhappy since the moment I met you," and then walk out? What did that say about him, the fact that he'd allowed not only days but months— and now years—to go by without revealing to her his real feelings?

No, he couldn't bring himself to do it—and even if he did, she'd just say no and go on pretending that they were still in a relationship, as if nothing had actually happened.

She was older. Maybe she would die first. Maybe he'd even get a few years to himself, eventually, three or four decades from now.

5.

During the fourth year of their relationship, she let him know that they were engaged and lifted her hand to show him the ring she had taken the liberty of buying on his behalf ("I have the receipt here; you can pay me back in installments if need be").

"We'll get married in the spring," she said. "I've always wanted a spring wedding."

But I don't want to be married to you at all, Gregory thought, although he said nothing.

A day later she arrived at the apartment with a huge stack of bridal magazines, and demanded he sit with her as she went through them one by one. He dutifully did. He even tried to make comments, until she made it clear that it was not his job to make comments. His job was merely to sit and listen, not to react.

Kill me now, he thought, as he had thought many times over the last four years.

"Oh, and look!" she said, finishing one magazine and lifting it away to reveal a blue flyer between it and the magazine below it. She passed it to him. A name he didn't recognize, dates, a location.

"What is it?" he asked.

"It's our artist," she said, and squeezed his hand. "The one you took me to on our first date. He's back in town—new show. We're going!"

All the way to the gallery she babbled on. It's the same artist! It's like renewing our relationship! *Is it the same show?* he wanted to know—or didn't want to know exactly, but felt he had to say something. But no, of course it wasn't the same show, she told him—how could it be? Don't be an idiot. But it would be even better! Just as their relationship had matured and become even better.

He felt a growing sense of dread. She held his hand, dragged him along.

And then they were there, going through the door. She had been right: it wasn't the same show as before, not exactly, though it was close enough. That same initial dark, narrow room. A series of hooks with dim shapes on them—a little higher on the wall. He thought: *Shirts.* But no, as his eyes adjusted, he realized that they weren't shirts after all—the shapes were wrong and they were too long. He reached out and touched one and found it soft and dry to the touch. Leather. Where was the card? There it was. *Skins,* it read.

He turned back to the hooks with a sort of wonder. It was like a series of men had peeled off their skins and then hung them up. Where were—but she was giggling, pulling him forward and out.

Another narrow room, without hooks this time, only a series of statues of men, complete except for the fact that they had been flayed. *No Skins,* read the card. Or maybe not statues after all. Were they real, the bodies preserved somehow? He wanted to think they were, although he didn't know why. Megan was still laughing and giggling and now had taken him by the hand again and was tugging him on. It was like she was not seeing what he was seeing, like she was in a completely different exhibit altogether. Or as if she had already decided what the experience was going to be and was enjoying that instead of what was actually there.

Her heels clattered against the floor as she walked. A third room, just as narrow. A sequence: hook with skin, body, hook with skin, body, hook with skin. Skin tingling, he moved toward the small white card. *Some Skins.*

Yes, he thought, *exactly.*

She was gesturing back to him, moving toward a door at the far end of the room, one with a metal bar in the middle of it. *Fire exit,* he thought.

"Come on," she said.

"Right behind you," he said, and when he took a few steps toward her, she pushed at the bar and opened the door. An alarm went off. Light poured in and then she was through. As soon as she was, he pulled the door shut from the inside. He was alone.

He heard the sound of her trying to open the door. A moment later she began to pound on it, calling his name. Slowly he backed away from the door and faced the skins, the bodies. He reached out.

She would find him eventually. He knew that, sure, he wasn't fool enough to think he was free. But for a moment at least he could pretend, could enjoy the glorious feeling of crouching alone beneath someone else's skin. Maybe it would give him something to look back on. Maybe it would give him enough to sustain him through at least one or two of the long and bitter years to come.

The Tower

I.

We called it a tower, though it was not a tower. It was, so the few remaining scraps of records seem to indicate, a fragment of a skyscraper, the tallest structure still standing from a city that had once been here, before the collapse, long before any of us were born. The tower that was not a tower was the only thing rising to any height above the rubble. Like a beacon, it drew stragglers in.

We lived in the rubble, coming and going through holes we had dug down into half-collapsed basements and subbasements. We grew fungi and mushrooms and caught the scattered, deformed vermin that still scuttled about. Sometimes we would leave our holes and make our way down to the water's edge and coax a twisted and listless creature or two out of the silty water by tickling its belly and then take it back and roast it over a fire. Only then—judging by the smell of it, the odor, whether it continued to move after what we thought was its head had been separated from what we thought was its body—did we decide whether we could bear to choke it down or if we would simply let it blacken and vanish into ash.

We felt the weight of the tower above us, even when we could not see it. We spoke about it often, about whether we should try to tear it down. If we tore it down, some of us believed, there would be fewer stragglers. But others pointed out that when stragglers came they always went straight to the tower, having glimpsed the glow illuminating its upper chambers. Once they went in, they rarely if ever came out again.

And besides, if we tore it down, we would have to reckon with Hrafndis.

Hrafndis had once been like us, scrabbling among the rubble, filthy and starved. She had her hole, which had been Angsdall's hole before a straggler took him. She struggled with the rest of us, cowered too when stragglers appeared.

And then one day someone wandered in, possessed of that look that stragglers have, the flesh blooming black across its chest. We barricaded our holes and watched it wander by, drawn to the tower. It came and halted at the tower's base, simply stared up.

This was before there was a beacon shining on the upper floor. It was Hrafndis who would later illuminate the beacon. Still, even without the beacon, stragglers would be drawn to the tower. One would come and stare and then, often as not, poke around at our holes. If we were unfortunate, it might drag one of us out and carry them off. If we were lucky, once it was tired of staring at the tower, the straggler either would simply wander past the holes without a second glance or we would manage to trap it beneath a deadfall trap, where it would remain, slowly writhing, for a year or perhaps two until, finally, it stopped.

This time we were not lucky. Or, rather, Hrafndis was not lucky. The straggler stayed there staring for a day, perhaps two, and then moved straight toward Hrafndis's hole.

It was clumsy, as all stragglers are, and quickly sprung the deadfall she had made. The rock tipped, but instead of falling and trapping it, the rock simply dealt the straggler a blow that propelled it the quicker into Hrafndis's hole and, once the creature was in, blocked the entrance.

We heard Hrafndis's scream, and then the sounds of her struggling in the darkness. She would soon be dead, we were sure, though she cried out from time to time for us to help her. After a while, we crept out from our own holes and stood listening. We even tested the stone that had fallen and determined that, yes, two or three of us straining together might roll it away. We could roll it away and then perhaps she could escape.

But we did not roll the stone away. By the time we had determined we could, we no longer heard her, and it seemed foolish to move a stone when a straggler roamed behind it. No, better, we reasoned, to simply leave things as they were, to let life run its bloody course.

A day went by, then two. One week, then several. Life returned to normal, if normal it had ever been. We forgot about the straggler, forgot about Hrafndis. Other stragglers came and went. We experienced a brief onslaught of creatures that might be said to resemble mice save for the unnatural number of limbs they had: seven. They were tasty, and could be eaten whole, when lightly seared over a fire.

And then, from one day to the next, they vanished and no new creature replaced them.

One day, one of us, Thurn, was moving through the rubble, remembering those mice that were not mice and searching for more, when he heard movement from Hrafndis's hole. Gripping the top of the stone that blocked the entrance were two hands, pale as bone, glinting. *The straggler,* he thought at first, though no straggler had ever had such hands as these, or even hands to speak of at all. And then, as Thurn watched, the hands flexed and strained and the stone cracked as easily as if it were a child's toy and Hrafndis stepped out.

She had changed greatly. She was bone white and covered with an almost translucent dusting of scale. Her features were severe and her bearing too was different. She walked in a jerky swaying way, as if she stood on stilts.

"Hrafndis," said Thurn. "You are alive."

When she spoke, Thurn told us before he expired, she moved her jaw in an unnatural way. Her voice when it came was the voice of someone who had not spoken in so long she had nearly forgotten how.

"No thanks to you," she whispered. Even these few words made her mouth bleed as if moving it was scratching it from the inside. And then she reached out and, in a single terrible movement, tore off Thurn's arm.

We were all brought out of our holes by the sound of Thurn's scream. Hrafndis had already turned and was walking away, moving in those awkward, measured steps toward the tower, the arm slung over her shoulder like a club or a gun, blood drizzling down her back. Thurn managed to babble what had happened and then died there on the ground. Hrafndis never looked back, simply walked to the tower and vanished into its base.

We buried Thurn, deep enough that stragglers would be unlikely to find him. We entered Hrafndis's hole, but it proved empty. There was no sign of the straggler that had been there with her, no waste or other residue. Indeed, the interior of the hole was immaculately clean and a little slick, as if it had been licked over and over.

II.

Once she entered the tower, she never left it. After a few years, we weren't certain she was even alive—or wouldn't have been had it not been for the light burning each night on the uppermost floor. And for what appeared at the tower's base.

At first, we saw only a glimmer, nothing distinguishable, and we kept our distance. But then, slowly, our curiosity got the better of us. We had not approached the tower earlier, even before Hrafndis took residence in it. Now we cast lots. The loser, it was determined, was to get closer and determine what they could about the glimmer, and about whether it was a threat to us.

I was the loser. Over the course of one long day I edged slowly closer to the base of the tower, ready to turn and flee at any instant. But when nothing moved, when nothing came after me, soon I became bolder. I moved forward until I could see clearly that the glinting thing was a metal statue of a man, standing at attention, stylized and nearly featureless.

Soon, I was beside it. I took a short length of pipe from the ground and prodded the statue with it, and suddenly the thing whirred to life. The pipe twisted free of my hands and flew end over end to thunk into the remnants of a concrete wall. It stuck there as if it were a thrown axe or an arrow from a bow. I turned to run but somehow the statue was already blocking my path, and I was unsure how to get around it while still staying alive.

Joints clicking, the statue extended its arms wide and began to walk slowly toward me.

Please, please, it said, though it had no mouth I could see. The words seemed to appear almost within my own head as if I were reading them. *You are welcome here. You are our guest.*

I looked behind me and tried to sidle to one side, but it was as if the statue had anticipated my movement. Slowly I was being coaxed deeper into the tower.

Please, please, the statue said. *Welcome! Welcome!* And then, *Did you call ahead? Did you? No matter, no matter. We shall find some way to accommodate you.*

It forced me deep into a large room, the one that filled the whole base of the tower. In the center were two crystalline shafts, tubes stretching up into the air to touch the ceiling ten meters above. At the bottom of each of these shafts was a little room. Slowly, with shooing motions, it ushered me into one.

The walls were of brushed steel, the only decoration a rectangular panel just inside the entrance, covered with circles numbered 1 to 16.

What floor? the statue asked. *What floor?*

"Floor?" I asked. I was unsure of what exactly it was asking or of what to say.

But apparently what I had said had been enough. It reached around the corner and into the little room and pressed the circle marked *4*.

A good trip, sir, said the statue, *a very good trip!* And then it turned and made its way back to the entrance.

After a moment, a brushed steel wall slid sideways to seal me in the room. And then there was a brief grinding noise and this wall slid back and revealed the chamber outside, exactly as it had been before. I pressed the circle marked *4* and the same sequence occurred again, nothing further. I waited for something more to happen but nothing did, and the next time I depressed the circle the little room remained as it had been when I first stepped into it: no closing wall, no grinding noise.

Eventually I stepped out of the tiny room again and, giving the statue a wide berth, made my way across the larger room and to a broken window. I climbed through it and made my way swiftly out, expecting the statue to again come to life and stop me. But it never did.

III.

Which was why, five years later, when the vermin ran out altogether and we finally decided we could not do without Hrafndis's help, I was sent to the tower. I had survived entering it when I was young, or at least younger. I was the only one, person or straggler, to enter the tower and come out alive. Didn't that prove I was chosen?

"No," I said, "it doesn't."

"Lucky then," they said, the others, the ones that were *us* but weren't *me.* "Lucky is enough. Lucky is all we have."

I could have resisted. I could have refused to go or could have pretended to go and then left the ruined city altogether. But to be honest, I was curious. And I figured perhaps she had realized that it was I, though too young to do much, who when she was trapped in her hole with the straggler had shouted, pounded on the stone, and tried to move it until the others dragged me away.

Was it I? I think it was. At least it seems that way to me now.

Besides, what sort of life did I have? Did I care to remain and slowly die of starvation along with the others? Perhaps she would kill me, though would that be much worse?

Near the entrance, I came across the same statue. It was on its side now, sleeping perhaps, or perhaps broken. I did not touch it, not wanting to tempt fate. I did not even step over it. Instead, I climbed in the window I had climbed out of before.

I entered one of the two small rooms at the bottom of the crystalline shafts, pressing the button as I had seen the statue do. Nothing happened. No grinding noise, no door closing. The same was the case with the other small room.

I decided to explore the base of the tower. It was a large, echoing chamber, empty except for two small rooms and the crystalline shafts. And yet, as I walked along its perimeter, I saw in the walls four indentations spaced evenly from one another, four compass points disrupting the edge of this circular chamber. One was indeed little more than an alcove and the one directly across from it was the same. But each of the remaining two, if you entered, had a lump the size of a fist upon its back wall that could be tugged upon to open a door.

I opened one and saw a flight of stairs zigzagging skyward. I climbed them, clambering upward, until the point where they abruptly broke off, the well that the stairs were in having partly collapsed. I prodded and poked at the rubble. It was soon clear to me that there would be no going further, and so I traced my way back down and tried the other door.

Here, I had better luck. The stairs broke off halfway up but were not fully blocked. I could scramble, crouched, up to where the stairwell was open again. Though there were no further stairs, there dangled the end of a rope, the strand knotted every yard or so all the way to the top. I got hold of it and pulled myself up, hand over hand, the wind whistling around me.

Halfway up I paused, dizzy. If she wanted to, I realized, Hrafndis could simply untie the rope before I reached safety. That would be the end of me. Still dizzy, I kept climbing, more rapidly now. When at last I reached the ledge on the top I rolled onto it and lay there panting, waiting for the world to stop spinning.

When I felt all right again, I stood and went to the door. I tried the handle and found it unlocked. For a moment, I almost opened it, then thought better of it. Instead, I softly knocked.

"Come in," she said immediately, no hint of surprise in her voice, no hesitation.

I turned the handle and went in.

She was in the first room, sitting in an ornate chair. She was even paler than I remembered from seeing her walk away brandishing Thurn's torn-off arm. And severe, as if she were made of bone rather than flesh and blood. From a closed door behind her came a noise like a straggler tearing another straggler apart. When she saw me, she smiled slightly, lips closed.

"I have been expecting you," she said. There was a strange warble to her voice, as though she were speaking underwater. As though she weren't used to it. To speaking.

"Expecting me?" I sat down. I kept my eyes on the door behind her. The noises had diminished somewhat but never completely stopped.

"To be honest, I expected you before now. You think because I live above you I do not know anything about you. But I do. I know everything. You've come here because you need help," she said. "All of you need help, and yet only you come."

"I was chosen to come, to represent the others," I explained.

"Just as you were chosen before to investigate my chem at the base of the tower," she said. "Why is it always only you?"

"Chem?" I asked. "Ah," I said, "you mean the statue."

She laughed, the noise high and birdlike, amused. "If you like," she said.

She stood and crossed to a table on the other side of the room. There was something wrong with the way she walked, tipping from side to side, her boots oddly deflated at the tips, as if her toes and a good part of the fore of her foot had been removed.

She took two porcelain cups from the tabletop, turned them upright, and filled them from a samovar resting at the table's center. Or, not a samovar exactly: something I did not have a word for. She brought me one of the steaming cups and returned with the other to her chair.

"Sit," she said. "Drink."

I did not sit, nor did I drink. She sat there regarding me, as motionless as a statue herself.

Finally, she moved. "You come asking something of me," she said, "and yet you will not accept my hospitality."

And so, knowing what I needed from her and not knowing how we could proceed with my doing otherwise, I finally sat, and sipped from the cup she had given me.

When she had finished her tea, she leaned down and placed the cup on the floor beside the chair. I did the same.

"I will be frank with you," she said. "I will not help them. They did not help me. Why should I help them?"

"We will die without you," I said.

"*They* will die without me," she said. "I did not say I would not help *you*." And then she smiled in a way that revealed her mouth to have more rows of teeth than I knew to be possible. "Though you might well regret how I do," she added.

I tried to speak, but I could not speak. I tried to stand but could not move.

"Please don't be concerned," she said. "It's temporary. It will wear off soon." She walked over to my chair and picked up the cup. "It was unkind of me to deceive you into drinking this tea."

A moment later I slid from my chair to the floor. My eyes were still open: I could see everything.

"It won't last long," she said.

I watched her legs approach, her boots. She teetered toward me, then began to drag me by the arms toward the door in the back of the room.

When she opened it, the noise inside grew louder. It still sounded like one straggler tearing another weaker straggler apart, though it was too dark to see anything clearly, to see what exactly it was.

She dragged me in. Abruptly the noise ceased. Then she smiled once, down at me.

"Soon it will wear off," she said. "Your extremities are, perhaps, already tingling. When sufficient time has passed, if you are still alive I will open the door and let you out."

She went out. Slowly she slid the door shut, bolted it from the outside, and left me in the darkness.

I was there for days, weeks perhaps, and the things that happened to me were far too terrible, are far too terrible still. There was light and noise, a flutter of wings that were not wings, a man screaming who both was and was not me. The press of other creatures tugging at my extremities, the seepage of one skin through another skin, the loss of most of one foot then the loss of most of the other, a man pounding on the door and begging in a voice not entirely his own to be set free.

But in the end, she was not the one to open the door. I was the one who opened it, breaking the door down as easily as she had broken the stone that had blocked her hole. I was not myself by that time, though in telling this I believe I have learned how to pretend to be myself again.

I broke the door down and came out intending to kill her. However, I did not kill her. Instead, upon seeing her, that desire faded, to be replaced by wonder. *Here*, I found myself thinking, *is perhaps the only other being in the world who can understand what I have become.*

And there we stood, bone white the both of us, regarding one another. The doorway opened behind me upon a room that was, now, immaculate, that looked almost as if it had been licked clean.

Which, indeed, as I knew all too well, it had.

We have not come down from the tower, she and I. That is not to say that others have not come up, even those I once knew, looking for food, looking for help. They have not come down from the tower either, albeit for other reasons entirely. You will not find them. Indeed, there is no sign they were ever here.

The Hole

1.

When the medical purser asked us when we had last seen Rurik,
we hesitated before responding. Not because we had something to
hide, but because we did not know at what point he would, to a
mind like hers, no longer be *Rurik*.

"Saw him alive, you mean," we finally said.

The interrogator nodded. "Alive," she said. "Moving."

This confused us further. Alive and moving were not the same
thing, at least not as far as Rurik was concerned.

"We . . . I'm not sure," we slowly offered.

She glanced at the security officer. He regarded his equipment
and gave a slight nod meant to be imperceptible to anyone but her.
It was not, however, imperceptible to me.

"Approximately," she said.

"Why, after my ordeal, am I being restrained?" we asked, although
we knew. "Why have you bound me? I will answer your questions
quite willingly. There is no need to restrain me."

"For your own protection," she lied.

"What do I need to be protected from?"

She chose not to answer this.

"Where have the rest of the crew gone?" we asked, although we knew.

"They are out searching for Rurik," she said. "And for you. Only a few more questions," she said, "and then I'll free you of the restraints." This, we suspected, was a lie.

"Fine," we said. "Ask your questions."

"How long ago?" she asked again.

"Two days ago, maybe three."

"A few days ago?" she said, surprised. "You must be mistaken. His recirculation system wouldn't have lasted so long. He couldn't have still been alive then."

"No?" we said, realizing our misstep. "Perhaps you are right. Out there, it is so difficult to keep track of time."

She looked to the security officer again and the man almost imperceptibly shook his head. "Where did you see him?" she asked. Her voice was harsher now.

We hesitated again, until there seemed no choice but to proceed.

"He was in a hole," we said.

"A hole." We nodded. "What kind of hole?" she asked.

"A deep one."

"He was alive?"

"What else would he be?"

Again, she glanced at the security officer, who this time neither nodded nor shook his head.

"When you saw him, in this hole, are you certain he was alive, yes or no?" she asked.

We hesitated yet again. How to answer? It depended, we supposed, on what she meant by *alive* and by *him*. Or what, for that matter, she meant by *you*.

We shrugged. "He was moving," we said.

2.

The hole was, as we would later tell the medical purser, a deep one, although it was more than that. It was the kind of hole one might not see until one was right on top of it, on the verge of falling in. I found the hole that way, or perhaps it found me, as I searched for Rurik, and before I knew it, I was at the bottom of it.

We had scarcely arrived, our engines hardly idle, when Rurik went missing. Nobody even knew he had left—one moment he was there and the next gone. Security footage showed him climbing into his gear, affixing his headpiece, and exiting through the hatch, and that was all. The tracking device that was part of his gear either had malfunctioned or had been deliberately disabled. He was simply gone.

The ten of us remaining debated what to do. Had he been acting strangely? Had there been any sign that something was wrong? Some thought yes, others no. But none of us in any case could bring ourselves to leave him. He was the captain after all. So, while the medical purser and the security officer remained with the vessel, the rest of us fanned out, searching for Rurik.

We each were assigned a direction and given an additional backup recirculation unit. I was to walk due northeast from the vessel, repeatedly calling Rurik's name. I was instructed to walk for two days, and then turn around and walk back. I was to keep my eyes open and if I saw anything that stood out against the gray landscape, I was to examine it to determine if it had anything to do with Rurik.

I set off. At first, I heard the other crewmembers also calling his name, the sound becoming fainter and fainter as we moved farther from the vessel and from one another. Probably, I believed back then, Rurik was dead, and we would never find him. He had a recirculation system that would last no more than five days. He had been gone two days already, and we had heard nothing from him. Something must have befallen him.

The landscape was gray, unvarying, the ground covered with a thick loam that absorbed the noise of my boots. My cries too seemed dampened despite being artificially amplified. There was, as there had been since we landed, a fog—not too thick but thick enough that after five minutes the vessel was only a vague shape behind me. Five minutes more, and it had vanished entirely.

I walked perhaps six hours. After the first hour, I was hoarse from calling Rurik's name, and from then on did so only intermittently. I saw little of note. Sometimes I would deviate from the path long enough to investigate a rare irregularity—a slight buckling of the earth, a strange rusted metal gear from who knew what sort of machine, a half-buried femur easily the length of my full body.

When it grew dark, I stopped. I unfolded a thermal blanket, wrapped it around me, and tried to sleep.

Did I sleep? Yes, I think so, and had dreams as well, though I have since come to question whether the dreams were in fact my own. In one, the creature possessed of the gigantic femur I had found loomed over me, sniffed at me, and then, rumbling, turned away. In another, I was Rurik himself, back aboard the vessel, hearing voices, always voices, no matter where I went. They whispered softly, too softly to hear, but an understanding was beginning to form nonetheless. The final dream (or at least the last one I remember) was the worst of all—me, as I was then, just then, Klim, alone, walking a straight line through an endless waste.

In the morning, I awoke with a start. I was stiff, my head foggy, and for a moment I knew neither where nor who I was. And then I was up, folding up my blanket, eating something sucked through the tube in my headpiece, checking again that my primary recirculator was affixed and still functional. Soon after, I started on my way.

I traveled perhaps five hundred meters when I realized that the ground directly before me was not ground at all, but a hole somehow nearly the same color as the ground itself. Before I could stop myself, I had plunged in.

For a time—I don't know how long—I was unconscious. When I came to, I was lying on my back on an irregular, lumpy surface, looking up at the smooth shaft rising above me, the walls so regular it was hard to believe they had been formed naturally. I examined my readouts. The recirculator was still there, unbroken, functioning. The spare one too was still in my pack, seemingly undamaged.

At first I thought, *How is this likely, that in the flatness and sameness of this place I manage to fall into a hole?* In all the time I had walked, it was the only hole I had glimpsed, and I had only glimpsed it as I was falling into it.

But such reflections were curtailed when I felt something beneath me move.

I scrambled quickly as far away as I could, which was not far. I groped for my weapon but didn't find it—I no longer had it. I turned on my light, and there, in the glow, was Rurik.

Or, rather, what was left of him. Both of his legs were broken, jagged bits of bone visible, the floor of the hole sticky with blood. His legs had begun to go black and were rotted through. If I hadn't been wearing my headpiece, no doubt I would have found the stench unbearable. His own headpiece was removed, lying shattered to one side. His body was far gone, livid where it wasn't outright black and suppurating. He hadn't moved, I told myself—he was well beyond the possibility of movement. The body must have simply shifted or settled under my weight.

I was still telling myself this when one of his eyes, the left one, swiveled toward me, the other eye moving in the opposite direction.

"Ah," he said through bits of broken teeth. "Klim. How nice of you to drop in."

I screamed. I cried for help. Of course, nobody came. I kept my distance from Rurik, and kept my eyes on him. Very slowly, he pulled his body up and dragged it until he was seated with his back against the shaft's wall.

When it seemed clear he intended no harm, I turned my back on him long enough to test the wall, look for handholds, a way up. The wall was smooth. There was nothing.

"Go ahead, Klim," he said once I turned back. "Test it for yourself. You will find there is no way out alone. Still, better for you to feel that you have tried everything before we strike a deal."

"You're not alive." I gestured at his broken headpiece. "You can't be."

"And yet we speak. But of course you're right. Technically, not alive."

It is difficult for me to explain what happened in the hours that followed. It is not the sort of thing one can understand without experiencing it oneself. At first I was incredulous: I had struck my head in the fall, I was still unconscious, imagining things. Or I was still five hundred yards back, asleep in my thermal blanket, dreaming.

"No," he said, though I had said nothing aloud. "You're not dreaming."

I was hurt then, legs broken, in the bottom of a hole, delirious.

"Your legs are fine," he said. "You had the good fortune of being able to use Rurik to break your fall."

In the hole he spoke like that, sometimes referring to himself in the third person, sometimes in the plural, more rarely just as *I*, as if he were sorting out who exactly he was and where he began and ended. Or as if he were speaking an unfamiliar language and trying to make sense of the eccentricity of a new logic of pronouns.

"I'm insane, then," I said. "I've gone mad."

"No, Klim," he said. "You're as sane as you've ever been."

We talked longer, for what else was there to do but talk? He spoke, often exactly as Rurik would, as if trying to prove to me that he was Rurik—or to himself perhaps. After a time, not knowing how to keep disbelieving what was happening to me, I entered into the spirit of it, and began to interrogate him about things only Rurik would know.

"There, you see?" he said at last, once he had passed my tests. "Do you have any doubt that this is Rurik?"

"But how can you be alive?"

He smiled, his lips splitting open. "As I already said, we are not alive."

"We?" I said. "Am I dead as well, and this is some kind of hell that we inhabit?"

He shook his head. "You misunderstand Rurik," he said. And then with some effort, "You misunderstand *me. I* am not alive."

"What is this place?"

He shrugged. "A hole," he said. "Simply a hole."

I stood and examined the walls again. "I have to find a way out of here," I said.

He shook his head. "You can't escape," he said. "Or at least you can't escape without me."

For a time, the dead man—if he was in fact dead and not merely not-alive (though what the difference between the two might be remained obscure to me)—continued to talk, a rambling patter that I could make little sense of. *What is a body but a body?* he asked. *And what does it matter what animates it? If memories are the memories of Rurik among others, who is to say we are not Rurik? In the way that you can make the pain of a toothache migrate from your tooth to your hand by digging your nails into your palm, so too so much that we see as stationary, flesh encased and immovable, is at heart profoundly fugitive.*

"I don't know what you're talking about," I said.

He sighed. At least I think it was a sigh. "You want to get out and I want to get out. In this body, these broken limbs," he gestured, "no, impossible. There is not much left of Rurik. But you, Klim. There is a great deal left of you. And you, I would venture to say, do not need all that is left. You are like a hole waiting to be filled."

"What are you saying?" I asked.

"Two brothers broke bread together and though it was not a meal sufficient for one, neither went hungry," Rurik said, offering a mutilated version of a tale that I had heard him tell before, back when he was the captain of the vessel rather than a not-living man in a hole. "I am asking you to share so that I can partake," he said.

"Share?"

"Just as, near the end, Rurik agreed to share. There is room," he said, and smiled. "You have so much extra room."

He had slipped down from the wall, and now he tried to push himself up again, the little flesh left on his hands sloughing away. He made it only partway and so leaned there as if about to pitch to one side, like an ill-made puppet, a doll.

"You know, of course, we can kill you," the limp Rurik creature said. "But we would prefer not to. We would prefer instead for you to invite us in. We can work together, serve one another. You can join us, and we can join you. It will be more pleasant for all of us, and more productive."

Pressed against the far wall, I said nothing.

"But of course, if you prefer to be killed, then we shall oblige you."

"And if I kill you?" I asked.

He laughed. "Good one, Klim," he said once he was done. "A very good one. How can you kill me when it has been so long since I was alive?"

I lasted several days. "Don't wait too long to decide," the Rurik creature cautioned. "Remember, you must have sufficient charge in your backup recirculator to make it back."

Or else, "We could be such friends. Such good, good friends."

Or later, "You think it must be terrible. This is simply because you can't imagine it."

Or later still, "You will say to yourself, do I prefer to die or shall I take this chance? Perhaps it isn't so bad. Perhaps it is better than being dead. And perhaps, even if it is so bad, I will one day escape."

Even if he was dead, even if I could not kill him, perhaps I could stop him from talking. And so, I charged at him and kicked him and kicked an opening in his side. From that hole came something long and whiplike, thin as ganglia yet strong and wiry. It wrapped around my wrist and then, when I tugged it free, split in two and took my other wrist as well. Each time I peeled it off and started to struggle free it further ramified and split. Soon it was wrapped about me tightly, like a net, and had brought me to my knees.

It held me there, facing Rurik, only inches away. He now looked purely dead, as if he had never been alive.

And then I watched one of the tendrils that held me unfurl and meander its way back to the body, feeling its way up it and into its nose, wriggling and pulsing deeper and deeper in, all the while never releasing its grip on me.

Rurik shuddered, opened one deflated eye.

"It's time," Rurik said. "You will join us. Shall it be willingly or no?"

3.

We had hoped to be able to retain the medical purser and the security officer intact, as a means of learning to interact properly with others of the species, and for this purpose had chosen to return to the vessel as if confused, claiming to have been lost, rejoicing to have found the vessel again at last. Even late in the game, we thought we might manage to convince them to untie us and accept us as human. But when they drew their weapons and began to threaten the Klim body, it seemed expedient to kill them. We have grown attached to the Klim body—perhaps because it is the only one of this species we have inhabited for any length of time while it was still alive. But perhaps it is more than that.

We extruded a part of ourselves, two parts of ourselves, and insinuated each of them, bringing what we could back to join what was already there: ourselves, then Rurik, then Klim, then finally the eight other crewmen we had reached out to, lured, and coaxed, one by one, down into the hole, and whose dead bodies we had possessed long enough to force them to climb on top of one another so as to allow us to climb out of the hole.

And so here we are, here he is, here I am, on this vessel, alone—if alone is the right word. Everything awaits him. From here, I can go anywhere.

As indeed we shall.

A Disappearance

I.

In late November, three weeks after his wife disappeared, Gerard sold their city apartment and moved to a small isolated house in the countryside. He had been planning to sell the house before she disappeared—or rather, *they* had been planning to sell, he quickly corrected: it had not been his idea, but *theirs,* he stressed, long before her disappearance. Together they had come over time to hate life in the suburbs, had begun to crave a *peaceful, simple life.* And so, they had made up their minds together to sell the apartment and buy a small isolated house in the countryside. They would take one last trip to the seashore, for old times' sake, and then they would sell their apartment and move. Was he to be blamed, he wanted to know, now that she was gone, for having proceeded individually as they had always meant to proceed together?

No, I said, by all means no. I wasn't blaming him for anything.

But of course, privately, I was blaming him. How could I not? It was he who had taken her to the seashore in the first place, setting in motion the sequence of events that would end in her disappearance.

It was he who had gone to the seashore with his much younger wife, and then he who had come back without her.

The details of her disappearance remained vague to him. One moment she was beside him in the surf and the next she was gone. He had, he claimed, run up and down the beach shouting her name, had even plunged chest deep into the surf and felt around for her. But she simply wasn't there.

"So, you think she drowned," I said.

"How do I know?" he asked. "Is she dead? Is she alive? Yes?" She could be dead, perhaps drowned, he admitted, a sudden wave dragging her far out to sea and into deep water. But maybe she was alive, abducted, taken by someone, suddenly, right from under his very nose. There was, after all, no body: there was always a chance she was still alive.

I shook my head. "It hardly sounds feasible," I claimed.

He regarded me for a long time, with that look of his that made me feel like layers of myself were being slowly peeled away, briefly considered, and discarded. Inside, I squirmed a little.

"No," he finally said, "probably not."

Like his wife, I too was much younger than Gerard, almost two decades younger. I had become friends with him only *because* of his wife, who had been my friend years before either of us met Gerard himself. We had grown up together, been in school together, and went everywhere together. We were often mistaken for being brother and sister. When people discovered that we were not in fact brother and sister, they would wonder if we were a couple, though when I would tell them we were old friends, that seemed to provide an explanation they could grudgingly accept.

Indeed, when Gerard first met the woman who would become his wife, he met me for the first time as well. His future wife and I were sitting at a table outside the Balmain, drinking, and when I excused myself to use the restroom, he approached our table.

"May I ask," he asked the woman who would become his wife,

"you can't possibly be serious about the fellow who just left the table, can you?"

"He's not my boyfriend," she said, promptly. "Simply a friend."

By the time I got back Gerard was sitting at the table, on the same side as her, touching her elbow lightly. I resumed my position across the table from her. Eventually, I left.

A month later they were married.

II.

On the day of the move, I, as one of Gerard's only friends, showed up. I was the only friend to show. Perhaps, with his wife having vanished under suspicious circumstances, I was his only remaining friend.

I helped him organize boxes and affixed to them the strips of colored tape that were meant to tell the moving crew where the boxes were to be placed in the new house. When the movers showed up, Gerard made the crew foreman listen while he explained each color of tape and what room it corresponded to. When he finished, the man grunted and picked up a box. "We'll move your boxes from one house to another," he said with a broad accent. "That's what we're paid to do." And then he left the room.

Nevertheless, we continued to arrange and label boxes. "But what if she comes back?" I asked at one point, mainly to see what Gerard would say. "What will she think when she finds you gone?"

He stopped and set down the roll of tape he had been using. It was a vague color—teal, he called it—only distinguishable from the blue tape if you looked at strips of both side by side. There was, I was certain, zero chance the movers would bother to do so.

"Well," he said slowly. "You're not moving, are you? I suppose, when she finds me gone, she'll come see you."

Perhaps I read too much into his answer, but it troubled me.

I stayed until the boxes were all loaded and the truck had started off. And then I stayed even longer, long enough to help him finish the dozen stubbies that he'd left in the fridge just for that purpose.

"You'll drive there tonight?" I asked, a little worried about how much he was drinking.

He shook his head. "No such luck," he said. "I'll sleep here, in the back of the car, and then drive down in the morning."

"In the back of the car?" I asked.

He nodded. "Yes," he said. "Why not?"

"Because," I said, "for starters, because it's a fucking car." After a moment, I offered, "Why not stay with me?"

But he simply shook his head. "No," he said. "I couldn't impose." And though I claimed it was no imposition, he still refused to accept.

We were each on our last stubby when he asked a question— not the question that I dreaded him asking, although still a question that I suspect he wouldn't have asked if he hadn't been drunk.

"You think I did it, don't you," he said. "That I killed her?"

I politely demurred, staring instead at the narrow mouth of my bottle, and yet he persisted. "Come on," he said, "you can see that all the rest of them think I did it. Why do you think they didn't show up today? So why did you? Don't you think I killed her?"

"I don't know," I claimed, "exactly what to think." And in saying this I was lying only slightly.

I didn't see him again for some time. By the time I passed the apartment building again the next morning his car was gone, and I thought, *Ah, well, better to just leave him alone in his isolated country house, and for you to forget about him, and him to forget about you.*

Months went by. Ten, maybe eleven. I had no word from him. He was living perhaps three hundred and fifty kilometers away, in the interior, somewhere near Goroke. I could, I told myself, forget about him, go on with my life as if nothing had happened, despite the loss of my real friend, his wife.

And then he chose to break his silence and contact me. It was a simple letter, sent in a paper-thin airmail envelope despite having only several hundred kilometers to go. I slit it open with a knife.

Come see me.

This was all, apart from an address and a telephone number.

I called the number. No answer. I called again, then again. Finally I had him, a strange connection, staticky in the extreme. "Hello?" he said. "Hello?" And then, despite the fact that I was already speaking, "Who is this? Is anybody there?" *It's me,* I believe I said, *your wife's best friend.* He didn't seem to hear me. "If this is some kind of joke . . . ," he said, and then hung up.

I will wait for a second letter, I thought. *When a second letter comes, I will trek out to see him.*

But no second letter came. A month passed, and then another. I sent a letter to the address he had provided in the letter, expressing my intention of visiting him, but there was no response to this either. When I called again, the number was no longer in service.

What do you do in such a circumstance, with a friend who is not, technically, a friend, who is only a friend because of your connection with his wife, who vanished? Who vanished under mysterious circumstances? Do you simply forget about him, let him fade slowly into oblivion? Do you think, yes, I'll contact him someday, only not yet? Or do you do as I did and instead take it upon yourself to show up at his door?

From the outside it looked ordinary, a small stone house that hadn't been updated for a century or perhaps more, but it was solid. I rapped on the door. There was no answer. I knocked again and called his name: *Gerard.* There was a long moment in which nothing happened, and I envisioned myself driving back the three hundred and fifty kilometers to the city without even having seen him.

And then the door opened. He stood there, blinking against the light, staring at me, no hint of recognition on his face. I said his name again and then, finally, his expression changed and he said,

"Ah, it's you." Turning, leaving the door ajar, he walked back into the shadows of the house.

Inside, it was a shambles. Despite nearly a year having passed, everything was still in boxes. Or, rather, piles of half-opened boxes were scattered throughout the rooms, with pieces of clothing, towels, draped over them. There was no bed that I could see—and when I asked him where he slept he gestured feebly to the garage. I went and opened the door and saw more boxes, whole crooked stacks of them, with all different colors of tape on them and, there, squeezed among them, a camp cot.

"What happened to your bed?" I asked. But he simply shrugged.

I followed him into the living room. He asked me if I wanted something to drink, and when I asked for water he went into the bathroom and came out with a glass smeared with toothpaste. He washed it in the sink and then brought it to me filled with silty water. Once I had finished it, he carried the glass back into the bathroom.

"What's happened to you?" I asked.

He shrugged. "My wife's gone," he said.

"That was almost a year ago," I said.

"I wanted to wait to unpack until she could decide where things would go."

"Gerard," I said, "she's not coming back."

"She might come back," he said. "She still might come back."

"No," I said. "Don't be a fool, Gerard."

He turned to me with that same look of his, the one that made me want to squirm. "What do you know about it?" he asked.

"Nothing," I claimed. "Nothing at all. But—"

"Do you mind if I ask you a question?" he interrupted.

III.

I of course knew what he was going to ask me. I'd been dreading it long before his wife's disappearance and had expected him to ask it well before now, but it had taken him being alone in the middle of the countryside, with nothing but his own mind for company, to bring himself to ask.

After I had killed him, I considered what to do with the knife. I had carried it for a year, perfectly happy to let him live as long as I felt I was not threatened. And yet I was always prepared, always armed. I would have to get rid of the knife. I was reluctant to do so, considering what else it had been used for, although I had no choice.

But first, before doing anything else, I had to sleep. I had driven nearly four hours, in the dead of night, to reach Gerard's house. I had hidden my car halfway down the dirt track, edging it into the tall grass, smearing the plate with mud. Better to take a slight risk and sleep a few hours before heading back.

So, I rolled his body facedown and went into the garage to rest on his camp bed.

As I slept, I had a dream. I dreamed about the time when all three of us were still alive: myself, Gerard, and his wife. Not about the month before his marriage or the few happy months after, but the time after that, when she came to tell me she had made a huge mistake, that she belonged with me, not him, that she hadn't seen it before despite how long we had been friends. Perhaps she hadn't seen it, she claimed, *because* we had been friends.

I was, both in the dream and in life, startled by this—I had long been in love with her, though thought she had no feelings for me. In both the dream and in life, I had succumbed: I became her lover.

But in the dream we had remained lovers. Gerard had eventually died—either of natural causes or we had killed him: the dream was unclear on that score—and then the two of us were together, happily ever after. We had a child, a son, and went on to enjoy a happy life.

Needless to say, actual life had turned out somewhat differently.

. . .

When I awoke, it was broad daylight. I rubbed my face. I would be wise, I told myself, to wait until dark before starting off. It would minimize my chance of being caught.

I got off the cot, stretched, and went from the garage into the house proper. He was still there, lying facedown on the floor, in his own blood. *It was a mercy,* I told myself. Flies were there now, buzzing all around him, and when I wasn't careful I began to hear a kind of susurrus in their buzzing, as if something was being whispered. *It's just a body,* I told myself, but in the end I retreated back to the garage.

Sitting on the edge of the cot, I thought about her. She had come to me, telling me that she and Gerard were going to the seaside. She told me I should come too, secretly, that she would find a way to slip out to see me. *Is that wise?* I asked her. But wisdom, of course, had nothing to do with it. And, of course, I went.

We had several good days together there, moments when she claimed to Gerard she was going to town or elsewhere and then instead trekked a kilometer up the beach to spend a few hours at my cottage. A moment even when she sneaked out in the middle of the night. Did Gerard suspect anything? I didn't think so, although that was of course one of the things I'd been wondering ever since she had vanished.

But no, I didn't think he knew, and it was clear from the way he finally posed the question, in the small stone house right outside of Goroke, right before I killed him, that if the thought of myself and his wife having an affair had crossed his mind, it had only recently done so, here, in Goroke, while he was alone with his thoughts. Or he had been good, at least, at presenting the matter at that moment as if this had been the case.

The question he asked me was, "Were you having an affair with my wife?" He asked in a way that made me think that the idea had only then occurred to him. The answer, of course, was yes, and I, of course, claimed no. And with indignation: how could he even think such a thing? But after that question, I knew other questions would follow, and before long he would figure out that not only had his wife vanished; she had vanished because I had murdered her.

It was the fourth day at the seaside, I think, our fourth encounter anyway, when she admitted to me that the reason she and Gerard had come to the seaside was because they were leaving the city, moving away.

"Moving," I repeated.

Yes, she said, to the country, a small house, to work on their marriage. They had recommitted to one another and were planning to start anew.

"This," I said, gesturing at the sheets crumpled around us, "is a funny way to recommit."

For a moment her brow creased, then it smoothed. "Oh," she said, "I thought you understood that this trip was the end. That this was me saying good-bye."

It was true, she had said that, and yet she had said it other times, so many times before: how was I to take her seriously? But now, finding that they were leaving, it did strike me that perhaps this time she was in fact serious.

What did I say to her? I don't recall exactly, except to remember a certain degree of desperation in my pleas, a certain amount of humiliation. She protested that she *didn't expect it to end this way*. I came to understand that she'd been expecting to have a final moment of glorious infidelity she could carry delicately back with her into her "recommitment" to her marriage. Things ended abruptly. Or, rather, they ended with her, tight-lipped, no longer saying anything, getting rapidly dressed and fleeing the cottage.

After she was gone, I lay in the bed for some time, staring at the ceiling. I was thinking. I was pondering the degree of my humiliation. I was wondering, if I waited long enough, would her marriage collapse? Would this final gambit go wrong and lead her back to me? I lay in that rented bed in that rented cottage and considered the shape of my life and saw many years of her occasionally stray-ing, momentarily departing from Gerard to seek consolation with me, but always going back to him. And, in my mind, even when he finally died, she did not come to me but found someone else, some-one more like Gerard. I realized I could not be with her nor could I escape her, that I was condemned to a sort of diminished life in which, slowly, over years and years, I would become nothing. That there would be no escaping this unless, somehow, I had the good fortune of her dying and freeing me.

And so, slowly, by bits and starts, my resentment and humilia-tion growing, I arrived at the idea of killing her.

It was a great deal easier than I thought it would be. I had a snorkel and a mask, and I waited hidden in the dunes down from where I knew their cottage to be. I waited an hour, perhaps two, and when I saw them step out of the door in their bathing suits I moved into the water and toward them. Before long, I saw beneath the waves the pale legs I recognized as belonging to her. I positioned myself with great care, and then, with a large crashing wave and a moment of distraction suggested in the flexion of the legs of her husband, as they both turned back to face the beach, I yanked her off her feet and below the water. She was too surprised to resist, and by the time she thought to do so, I was drawing her away, keeping her under, not allowing her to breathe. She struggled, once almost escaped. She managed to claw my mask down around my neck. However, the act of seeing my face and realizing who it was proved more of a shock to her than the mask had been, and I managed to keep the snorkel in my mouth long enough that before I ran out of breath she was dead, drowned. And then, leaving her body to drift, I reaffixed the mask, cleared the snorkel of water, then dragged her slowly out to sea, taking her body to the edge of the reef. I slit her throat open with my knife, the same knife I would use a year later to kill her husband. I watched the blood that would draw the sharks to her slowly bloom and then released her corpse and allowed it to sink gently into the darkness.

I returned that day to the city. I was there, waiting, when Gerard came back, bereft, unsure of what had happened to his wife. I was there to comfort and reassure him, though, above all, to reassure myself that he did not suspect me. After all, I could not know for certain what his wife had let slip about our relationship.

But for a long time I was convinced he knew nothing. There was only that gaze of his, those brief moments of thoughtful consideration as he looked at me, that left me unsure. Which had led me here, to this cot in this garage, staring at the door that led into a room containing his dead body.

I did my best to clean up after myself. I rubbed a damp cloth over every surface, obliterating my fingerprints. I lit a fire in the fireplace and then turned the gas on low on the unlit stove just before I left for good. I got in my car and drove at a stately, leisurely pace back to the city. By the time the place caught fire, I was kilometers away.

I have been here ever since, unsuspected, alone, bereft now of not just one friend but two, both of whom I betrayed. Do I regret it? No. And then again, yes. In truth, I do not know what I feel, though I do know that often at night I dream of them, of their deaths. Of the slow seepage of her blood into the salty water. Of the sharp spurt of his against the stone wall as I slit open his throat. I lie and dream, and wake to hear the blood beating in my own ears, and wonder, *Could this have turned out any differently? Could we all still be alive? Happy even?*

But no, I think, once daylight starts to break. Things could only have turned out this one way, only exactly as they did.

The Cardiacs

He opened the box, propping its lid with a stick, and then slipped his hands in. The top of the lid, facing us, was lacquered black, a semicircle of bounding hearts painted on it. We watched his head and chest, his twitching shoulders, his empty and unblinking gaze. Where his hands had gone, his arms soon followed. When, finally, he removed them, they were soaked in blood to the elbow.

When did we realize something had gone wrong? I can speak only for myself: I believed even then that it was all part of the act, done for effect. Even when, as he continued to stare at his dripping hands, the five volunteers clutched their hearts and collapsed one by one on the stage, I still believed.

For a moment more he was stock-still. And then he turned, hands still suspended directly before his eyes, and regarded through the gaps between his blood-thickened fingers the heaped volunteers. Slowly, so as not to alarm us, he turned back to the box and climbed in. He kicked the stick out and the lid slapped shut.

After minutes of silence and stillness, we climbed onstage and opened the lid. We found the box empty and slightly damp inside, as if it had been licked clean. No trace of blood, nor any trace of him.

Long after we buried the volunteers and burnt the box to cinders, it was all I could do not to believe, not to feel him there, just behind me, always about to reappear.

Smear

1.

Aksel could see a smear, something just inside the vessel's skin. He blinked, rubbed his eyes. It was still there.

"Query," he asked. "What am I seeing?"

The voice responded, *I cannot know what you are seeing. I can only know what you are looking at.*

"All right," he said. "What am I looking at?"

The voice did not respond. Why did the voice not respond? Surely it knew what he meant. And then he remembered.

"Query," he said. "What am I looking at?"

The voice responded immediately, *Bulkhead.*

"No," he said. "There's something there, something more."

The voice in his head responded, *Interior of your faceplate.*

"No," he said. "Not that either." He called on the vessel to remove his helmet, which it did by extruding a chrome claw from a bulkhead and plucking it deftly off his head. *Why did it do that?* he wondered. *It could have done it just as easily by deploying a focused magnetic field.* Was the vessel trying to unsettle him?

He looked again. The smear was still there, just in front of the bulkhead, a few inches away from it, over his head, perhaps a meter long, a half meter wide. He reached up and tried to touch it, but, strapped down as he was, couldn't reach. "Query," he repeated. "What am I looking at?"

Bulkhead, the voice insisted.

"No," he said. "Between myself and the bulkhead."

For a long time the voice said nothing. Had he gotten the form wrong? He didn't need to say *query* again, did he? But then, finally, hesitantly, the voice spoke.

Are you looking at the object properly? Is your gaze centered upon it? If your gaze is not centered upon it, you are no longer looking at it. You are merely remembering it.

He instructed the vessel to reposition his chair until the smear was centered in his vision. He focused his eyes on it. He held his gaze steady, unblinking.

"Query," he repeated. "What am I looking at?"

Bulkhead, the voice said.

"No," he replied, irritated. "In front of the bulkhead."

There is nothing between your eyes and the bulkhead.

But it was there, he could see it. A smear, semitransparent but certainly present. He was sure he could see it. What was he seeing?

I can tell you what you are looking at, the voice said, unbidden, *but not what you are seeing.* Which made him wonder if the voice had burrowed deeper into his head than he had realized and could hear what he was thinking.

2.

Apart from the vessel, apart from the voice, he had been alone for a very long time. He had been strapped into the vessel and then the vessel had been accelerated to a tremendous rate, albeit very gradually, over the course of days, so as not to kill him.

The chair had been made so that he would never have to leave it until he left the vessel for good. The chair was now so integrated with his body that it was hard for him to remember where body stopped and chair began. When he awoke, he felt as if he didn't have a body. It was a tremendous effort to move a digit, let alone a limb.

When he awoke, the vessel displayed on the inside of his faceplate a countdown of the months, days, minutes, and seconds before deceleration would begin.

Off, he whispered, and the vessel reduced the countdown to a red pixel.

Why was he awake? Was he meant to be awake? He was still groggy, still woozy. Maybe he wasn't awake at all but only dreaming. He wasn't meant to be awake in the vessel, ever.

Why am I awake? he whispered, and immediately there were words in front of his eyes, as if the faceplate had been written on. It was the vessel, responding.

Unexpected failure in storage system, the words read.

What failure? he asked.

Storage system component 3/9aOxV.

Excuse me? he said. Upon which the vessel displayed a series of schematics that made no sense to him at all.

So, he would remain unstored for the rest of the trip. Would he die? The vessel indicated he would not die: it would feed him intravenously through the chair, converting the molecules of extraneous portions of itself into nourishment. Would he waste away sitting in the chair? The vessel indicated no, it would continue the stimulation of muscles and nerves that it had been conducting while he was in storage. Which meant that his body was constantly twitching, his muscles bunching and releasing, though he was not the one doing it. It was being done to him.

He asked the vessel for a distraction. It opened a feed to his faceplate and showed him space around itself, mostly black, a few specks of light. He asked if it had music or some sort of teleplay. As it turned out, no, it didn't. He was never meant to be awake—nobody was ever meant to be awake on the vessel. The vessel could show him space. The vessel could show him schematics.

Perhaps if he told it stories, he hoped, it could learn to tell them back.

Indeed, it did tell them back: verbatim each time. When he instructed it to construct its own stories, it offered a mishmash of what he'd already told it, repurposed in a way that made little sense.

And so, instead, he regarded schematics, examined a representation of space on the inside of his faceplate, traced the curve of the bulkhead with his eyes. He slept, woke, slept. He never ate, but, fed intravenously, was never hungry. At least not at first. He watched his body grow lean, hardly an ounce of fat left. His suit draped loosely on him.

Are you sure I'm being fed enough to survive? he asked.

Technically speaking, the vessel responded, *you are being fed enough to survive.*

The voice manifested after several weeks of being awake, alone. At first, he sensed it more than heard it, had a strange inkling that something was there, speaking to him—or, rather, trying to speak to him. Was it the vessel? At first he thought yes, it was the vessel. But they didn't talk quite alike. And when he asked the vessel about the voice, it seemed baffled.

For some time—days, even weeks—he simply listened. He taught himself to filter out the noise of the vessel around him and just wait, listen. It was as if the voice was there, slightly beyond a frequency he could hear, making his eardrums throb slightly but not in a way that conveyed sense. He spoke to it, tried to coax it to speak back until, suddenly, to his surprise, it did.

It had rules, formulae that must be followed, patterns of speech it seemed prone to respond to. He stumbled onto them only slowly and gradually. It would not always tell him what he wanted to know. There was still much he didn't know.

3.

Vessel, he whispered, *please replace my helmet.*

The same chrome claw on a long pale arm plucked the helmet from the floor with surprising delicacy and pushed it back onto his head. When it was affixed, he looked again for the smear through the faceplate. It was still there, still visible. It didn't matter what the voice claimed.

He asked the vessel about the smear.

There is nothing there, the voice said again, despite his not following discourse protocol. *I already told you.*

"I wasn't speaking to you," Aksel said. "I was speaking to the vessel."

But the vessel did not respond. The faceplate in front of his eyes remained blank.

"Have you disabled my interface?" he asked.

There was no response, either from vessel or from voice.

"Query, have you disabled my interface?" he asked.

Query, the voice responded. *What is an interface?*

Interface, interface. What an odd word, he told himself. *Intraface* would mean inside the face, within the face, which made sense. But *interface* would mean between the face. What could that possibly mean: between the face?

"Query," he began, but the voice immediately cut him off. *Don't ask,* it said.

It had a tone now . . . Did it have a tone? Had it had that mocking tone before? What was the voice? What did it have to do with him? Why was he willing to listen to it? Why hadn't he panicked?

But no matter how he tried to work himself up he couldn't bring himself to panic. Maybe the voice was doing that to him too.

His arm was little more than a stick wrapped in skin. Looking at it, it didn't look like an arm that could possibly belong to him. In fact, the more he looked at it, the less it looked like an arm at all.

But when had he taken his suit off? Why was he looking at a bare arm at all? And why, if he wasn't wearing his suit, was he wearing his helmet?

Or wait. *Was* he wearing his helmet?

His gaze slowly slid to the smear and then wandered away. If he looked at it out of the corner of his eye, it almost made sense, almost looked familiar. He tried to look at it and not look at it at the same time, but, like the voice had been at first, it felt as if he could almost sense something but not quite. As if whatever it was had impinged on this world by accident, was only being seen because of an anomaly.

What if that anomaly is me? he wondered.

Or was that the voice wondering it?

Perhaps, if he got closer. Perhaps, if he regarded it from one side, at an oblique angle.

Vessel, he whispered, *move the chair forward.*

But the chair didn't move. The vessel was paying him no heed. Perhaps, as with the smear, it no longer realized he was there.

He kept looking, kept staring. Part of him felt the smear was staring back. Watching him. Was it staring back? No. It was only a smear; a smear couldn't stare.

If he could only get closer, move a little nearer, then he'd see it clearly, he was sure. Almost sure.

Time went by. Years, maybe, or what felt like years. When he regarded his arm again, it still didn't look like an arm. When he lifted the claw on the end of it and touched the release and kept pushing until the belts restraining him actually parted, it looked even less like an arm.

It took tremendous effort to free himself from the chair. And more effort still to crawl across the deck. Still more to turn and look upward, to regard the smear.

Was it still there? Yes, it was still there, only differently distended from this angle. It was, almost, a face. It was, almost, a human face. He crawled a little closer, looked up again. Still smeared, still distorted, though anamorphically transformed. Yes, a face. Maybe. He crawled until his head was touching the surface of the bulkhead and then looked up again. Yes, a face, a face very much like his own—his own face in fact. He stared into it, filled with wonder.

After a moment the face smiled, tightly, in a way that bared its teeth.

Or would have bared them if what was inside the mouth were teeth.

4.

They scanned the small craft. Nothing harmful detected, no extraordinary presences, nothing to give pause. Out of caution they kept the craft quarantined, alone at its dock, for several weeks, before finally sending a team in.

The man was out of his chair, eyes wide open, staring at the upper portion of the vessel's bulkhead. He had been torn free of the chair and his legs were tangled with a snarl of tubes and wires, many of which were still attached to his body. A discolored spill of dried fluid spread in a trail behind him. His neck was bent impossibly upward, his body desiccated and bloodless.

"Where's his suit?" asked one of the technicians.

The other shrugged. "I don't know," he said.

"What's with his arm?"

"Arm?" said the other. "Is that what that is?"

It was contorted, and little more than bone. He reached out and pushed down on the arm with his boot. The body yawed to one side, hollow or nearly so. When he drew his boot back, the body rocked back and forth, slowly settling onto the floor.

He grunted. "What do we do with him?"

"Incinerate him," said the other.

"And the craft?"

There was a long moment before the other responded. "No reason to destroy that," he finally said. "We can salvage it."

But he wasn't looking at the other technician as he said it. Instead, he seemed to be looking at a spot high up the bulkhead, near the curve where wall became ceiling. He took a step forward and reached his hand out through the air, as if to touch something. Then he drew back and stared at his gloved hand.

"What is it?" asked the other.

"Nothing," he said, confused. "I thought I saw something. My . . . faceplate must be dirty."

The other nodded. He started for the airlock. When he realized the first wasn't following, he stopped, looked back.

"Coming?" he asked.

"Just a moment," said the first. He had pulled one arm from its sleeve and back into his suit and now had it pressed between the suit and his chest. He worked the fingers up past where the suit joined the helmet, trying to rub at the faceplate from the inside.

"Come on," the other insisted.

"You go ahead," the first managed to say. "I'll follow you out in a moment."

All alone, he stood there, hand caught between his throat and the rim of the helmet, waiting. He had seen something, he was sure. Or almost. A swath, a fluttering, something almost visible.

What was it? he wondered.

Or not quite that: *Query: what was it?* he wondered. Yes, that was what the thought had been. What a strange way to think.

He wriggled his fingers, swallowed. He waited, listened.

—for Rex Marshall

The Glistening World

1.

There came a moment late in the evening when Dawn realized that someone might be following her. Or not *realized* it, exactly—she'd had enough to drink to have a hard time putting things together as precisely as that—but just that she kept seeing the same man wherever they went.

"There's that guy again," she said to her friend Karin.

"How do you know it's the same one?" Karin asked, voice slurred. "Maybe it's two guys who look alike."

"No, no," Dawn said, "it's that same guy, the one in the gold suit. How many guys in a gold suit can there be?"

"Gold suit?" said Karin. "I haven't seen anyone in a gold suit."

And, true, when Dawn looked around he wasn't there anymore. But he had been there, wearing a gold suit. And he had been there earlier, too, at the previous bar. Never close to her, never all that close, never looking at her, not really, always looking away so she could only see the glistening suit and the back of his head. Mostly he was not there, but every once in a while when she looked around, there he was.

...

They went on to the next bar. When she was out with Karin, this is what they did: went from bar to bar, drank, waited, watched. Sometimes other people talked to them, sometimes not. They each sat on a stool and ordered a drink. When that drink was gone, they went on to the next bar.

There he was again, glistening, facing away, partly hidden in the crowd. He was bobbing his head slightly, maybe singing along to the blaring music, maybe not. She couldn't see his face, so couldn't tell. He wasn't talking to anybody, was just standing there. She pawed at Karin's arm, trying to get her to turn around and look, but Karin was talking to someone, a man, older, not unhandsome, a little cagey, and wouldn't be distracted. When she finally did turn, the man in the suit was gone.

"It was him again," Dawn said.

"The gold suit guy?" Karin made a pretense of looking around. "Are you sure you're not seeing things?" she asked, and then turned back to continue speaking with the man on the stool next to her.

Maybe I am *seeing things,* Dawn thought. After all, nobody in this bar was dressed up, no men were wearing even business casual. Why would someone be wearing a golden suit here?

Leaving Karin still talking, she slid slowly off her stool, making her way across the room to where she had seen the man in the gold suit. He wasn't there, no sign of him. Was there a back room? No, didn't seem to be. Wouldn't he have had to come right by her to leave? *Maybe I am imagining it,* she thought again.

"Excuse me," she said to two women standing near where she had last seen him. "Did you notice a man in a gold suit?"

"A gold what?" said one.

"Is this some kind of joke?" asked the other. "Do I know you?"

Slowly she wove her way back to her stool. By the time she arrived, Karin was gone.

Maybe Karin was in the bathroom. Maybe she'd be back any minute.

When she wasn't, Dawn tried calling her, but Karin didn't pick up. She texted her, waited for a reply. It wasn't like Karin to simply leave. She ordered another drink, sipped it.

About halfway through, someone sat down beside her at the bar and nodded slightly. A man, older, his breathing ragged. He wasn't exactly handsome, though he wasn't ugly either. He looked almost like the guy Karin had been talking to earlier. Was he?

"What are you drinking?" the man asked.

"Were you here earlier?" she asked. "Talking to my friend?"

He looked confused, unsure of what answer she expected. Like there was a right and a wrong answer. But there was no right or wrong answer—she just wanted the truth.

And then he decided on a strategy. "I don't know," he said in a voice that was meant to be coy. "Was I?"

Immediately she got up and left.

She walked on to the next bar. She looked for Karin inside, and when she didn't find her went to the next bar. After that, there were no more bars, so she walked back, thinking she would check each of the bars in reverse order until she found her friend.

She would have, too, if she hadn't seen, far down the block, the man in the gold suit. There he was, the back of his suit, the back of his head, walking away, unless it was someone else. But how many men in gold suits could there be in one city? No, she thought, it wasn't someone else, it couldn't be.

She followed him. It was late, the bars still crammed with people but almost nobody outside on the street. He was walking quickly. To keep up with him she had to occasionally break into a jog.

She moved swiftly past the windows of the remaining bars, through the puddles of light and noise coming through their half-open windows and doors, until she was on quieter, darker streets, the noise and light fading behind her. He was still there, a little way ahead. There were fewer streetlights now and she couldn't always see him glistening.

What am I doing? she wondered. *This is dangerous.* But she kept following him.

And then he slowed, or she sped up, or both, for there he was right in front of her, almost close enough for her to touch him. How could she have gotten so close without realizing? Was she that drunk? There she was, reaching out, her fingertips brushing the smooth cool fabric stretched across his back, then reaching further still to grasp the man by the shoulder.

He stopped walking, turned to face her. Or would have, if he had had a face. There was only a smoothness where a face might be.

This was shocking enough, but then, somehow, he smiled. And for someone to smile without a face was more shocking still.

2.

What happened next? She wasn't sure. How could she be sure? Because when he had smiled like that, in a way that, faceless, should have been impossible, it had felt as though a part of her, the part able to think, had fled. What was left of her just had a series of scattered impressions, things she couldn't quite make rational sense of, couldn't quite link up.

During that time he hadn't touched her. Instead, he just looked at her—or not *looked* exactly, since he didn't have a face: he directed his head in her general direction and then began to walk backward, away from her. She, as if hypnotized, followed.

The way he walked was too smooth, without hesitation. Impossible to do, if you couldn't see where you were going. She began to wonder if he did have a face after all, but a face that was on the wrong side of his head, hidden there, under his hair.

He walked backward, down one street and then down another, without hesitation, as easily as if he could see where he was going. Perhaps he had memorized the route. He moved to a doorway, still walking backward. He pressed himself against the door and put his hands behind his back. She heard the sounds of him working the lock. A moment later the door swung inward.

Behind him was a cramped entryway, a set of stairs. He glided up them, still walking backward. He moved along the hall at the top of them, and she followed. She walked past office doors with pebbled glass windows, company names gilded on them. And then he stopped at what seemed a bathroom door, a stylized image of a human figure on it. He held the door open and ushered her in.

She had to duck under his arm to get in the door. Inside, the light was dim, the room almost in darkness. She had entered expecting him to follow her, but he hadn't followed. He let the door swing slowly shut instead, leaving her alone.

When her eyes adjusted to the dimness, she realized that she wasn't in a bathroom at all. She wasn't sure it was, properly speaking, a room. The walls weren't straight but instead bowed, and seemed to flex and relax, as if the room, if it was a room, was breathing. She turned to go out, only to find there was no door to go out of: the wall behind her was as smooth and blank as the man in the glistening suit's face.

Dawn held still, her head swimming with alcohol, and waited. She waited. *Something has to happen,* she told herself. *Eventually something must happen.* When nothing did, she sat down and crossed her legs.

Maybe she slept a little, or maybe she simply stared. Eventually, aware again, she began to believe there were shapes flitting around her, whirling and insubstantial, but becoming more substantial the more attention she paid them.

For a long time these shapes were just vibrant colors melding and clashing. Then either they became sharper or she did: it dawned on her that what she was seeing were human figures. She watched one glide across the space in front of her, slightly off balance, then another follow and catch up with the first, wrapping it in an embrace. The first figure turned and met the embrace, or seemed to, but then it either fell back or was pushed away, the second figure falling on top of it. And then the two figures were writhing, one atop the other. *Karin got lucky,* she found herself thinking, though she was not sure what had made her think the figure was meant to be Karin.

And then, a moment later, she realized that she had spoken too soon, that what she had thought was an embrace had never been an embrace at all, but one figure destroying another.

She cried out. The figures paid her no heed, one because it was already motionless and spreading in a broad puddle of light across the floor, the other because it couldn't hear her. She stood and pounded on the wall, if it was a wall, and screamed to be let out, but there was no answer. She felt the wall, searched for the door, trying not to look at the figures as they regrouped and acted out the same sinister pantomime over again. After a while, she put her head between her knees and tried to breathe, tried to think, tried to understand what she could do.

And then, in a moment of inspiration, she stood, moved to the center of the room, and, as naturally as possible, walked backward, toward the wall. She felt behind her with both hands and there it was, the handle, and she pulled on it and a moment later was out the door.

3.

Which was why she knew before finding her body that Karin was dead, why she didn't respond with shock or alarm when, a few minutes later, she stumbled backward out of the bathroom that was not a bathroom, made her way the half dozen blocks back to her car, drove to Karin's house, and discovered the body of her friend stabbed to death on the floor. But she had called the police when she was still several miles from the house. She knew. She already knew.

She didn't tell the police this. She didn't tell the police any of it. No, for the police, she claimed it was simply a matter of Karin disappearing while they were out and her searching for her, looking everywhere, and finally going to her house.

But what, she kept wondering as she talked, *if I had gone to Karin's house to look for her rather than following the man in the gold suit?*

Would she have been able to save her friend? No: instead, both of them would be dead. She was sure of it.

Indeed, for months after, when she closed her eyes, she would see that man in the gold suit, moving perfectly backward, looking at her despite not having a face, luring her away from her own death.

Wanderlust

That first time, when Rask had first felt the urge, he'd had a good job, a delightful girlfriend he was engaged to marry, an excellent apartment. He had been at work, sitting in his cubicle, typing up a quarterly evaluation of his section, when he felt someone watching him. He turned but nobody was there.

He turned back, continued with his report. A moment later he felt it again, the hair rising on the back of his neck. This time he turned quickly, whipping his head around—still, nobody there. Could it be one of his fellow workers? No, none of them were looking this way. Or they were looking out of open curiosity, wondering why he had spun around so quickly, what was the matter with him.

He got up and went to the bathroom. He stood in a stall, door closed, and stared at the little coat hook on the back of the door. He waited. Did he still feel the gaze behind him? No.

He flushed the unused toilet for form's sake. He splashed water on his face at the sink. There he was in the mirror, looking as he always did, a little more haggard perhaps, slightly exhausted, but still recognizably himself, still Rask. He stayed there, meeting his reflection's gaze, hesitating.

And then he felt it again: that prickling of somebody else's gaze on the back of his neck; the unavoidable feeling of being watched. In the mirror, he examined the line of closed stall doors behind him. There were no feet below any of them, no movement, no sign of human presence, and yet he still felt watched.

He tried to shake it off. He splashed water over his face again. He returned to his desk and quickly drank the rest of his coffee, and then felt the blood vessels pulsing in his eyes. He still felt watched. There was a video camera affixed to one corner of the ceiling, but it didn't work, never had—the light wasn't on, he could see where the power line had been cut—nevertheless, he waited for a moment when he thought he was unobserved and taped a piece of paper over the lens. But this didn't make him feel any less observed.

He waited until everyone else had left and then sat there, alone, just him. He still felt watched. He prowled the floor of the office, just to make sure. He turned off all the computers, every one in every cubicle. He put the pictures of family members and boyfriends and girlfriends facedown on the desks. He unplugged the radios and boom boxes and put them into desk drawers. And then he went back to his desk and sat, fingers poised over the keyboard as if he were about to type something, even though the computer was not on. He waited.

A moment later, he felt it.

This is crazy, he thought. *I'm being crazy.* But thinking this didn't make him feel less watched.

At home his girlfriend was sitting at the table, arms crossed.

"I didn't know if I should eat or wait," she said. "And so, I waited."

"You should have eaten," Rask said.

"I thought you'd call me if you were going to be late," she said. "Usually you do."

"I didn't know how late I was," he said. "I lost track of time. I'm sorry."

They ate lukewarm lasagna. After dinner, she spread some catalogs on the table. She asked Rask what he thought of this wedding dress or that wedding dress, this table setting, that technique of folding a napkin.

"Fine," he said, half ignoring her. "Yes. Good. Good."

"What's wrong with you tonight?" she finally asked.

But that was a question that Rask didn't quite know how to answer. *Someone is watching me,* didn't sound right, nor did, *I keep imagining that I'm being watched.* The truth was somewhere in between these things, though where exactly, and how to define it in a way that she would understand, he wasn't sure.

She was still staring at him, waiting for an answer.

"I'm just tired," he finally said.

That night, lying beside her, staring up at the ceiling, he felt even more strongly that he was being watched, and slowly he felt panic begin to rise. He put up with it as long as he could and then got out of bed. His girlfriend moaned a little but did not wake up.

He went into the living room. He tried to sit and read, but still he felt it. He stood and began to pace, moving from one side of the living room to the other, and felt a little better, if only for a while. When he extended his route into the kitchen, that helped, though that too, in time, didn't feel like enough. Before long, he found himself opening the door into the hallway, striding out of his apartment and down to the elevator and back, and then, before he knew clearly what he was doing, he was dressed and walking down the emergency stairwell and out the door, up and down the streets near his apartment, and then up and down streets a few blocks away, and then out into the city beyond.

II.

Thus began for Rask what he would refer to later, after his institutionalization, as his days of wandering. He went from city to city, never staying more than a week at a time, begging or stealing food, sleeping under bridges or in parks, moving along whenever he felt again that he was being observed. *Was* he being observed? He didn't know, just as he hadn't known the first time, but he felt something, thought he felt something, and that was enough to make his anxiety rise. The only thing that would alleviate the anxiety was to move, to walk and not stop walking, to wander.

As he went from city to city, his face and hands becoming sun- and wind-chapped, rough, the soles of his shoes wearing thin, his clothing becoming sweat stained and stinking, he began to see the world in a different way. He had been in dozens of cities, and the more he visited, the harder time he had seeing them as distinct and separate. They struck him as more and more alike, as if parts of the same city were being rearranged and used over again. He would see an alley and think *Chicago*, even though he was in Nashville. But it was, he was sure, almost sure, the same alley he had seen in Chicago. A freeway overpass in Salt Lake City and one in Albuquerque not only looked alike but also seemed to be, the more he thought about it, exactly the same. There were even moments when he would see someone discard something into a dumpster—a broken brooch, a bag of family photographs, a top hat with a hole punched through the top of it—and when he opened the dumpster would find nothing there at all. And yet, opening another dumpster days later, in an entirely different city, there the things were, waiting for him.

Every place is one place, he began to feel. For a while this seemed like mere theoretical knowledge and then, unexpectedly, it seemed like much more than that. He became convinced that, if he could bring himself to believe, he would be able to navigate from these bits and pieces of places back to the places where they had originated. He could enter a dumpster at West 180th Street in Hudson Heights and emerge behind a nightclub in South Beach. All he had to do was keep fixed in his mind the place where he had originally seen the piece of the other city. He would close his eyes, move forward, and when he opened them he would be elsewhere.

But even when this actually started happening, a part of Rask held back. Was it really happening or was he simply imagining it? Cities didn't really work like that, did they? Was he doing it all himself? Was he allowing days to pass in a kind of fugue state while he hitchhiked his way from one city to another? But any time he started to feel a presence again, any time he began to feel watched, he would search out these flaws in the city's fabric and, when he found them, use them to go to another city.

Sometimes he considered his life: what it had been, what had become of it. He had left, he thought sometimes, for no reason. And now he was wandering for no reason. He had given everything up—his job, his girlfriend, his life. But any time he began to feel this way, he would quickly begin to feel eyes on him again. And then he would think, *No, I was right to leave. What else could I have done?*

And so it went on, with Rask moving from city to city, either on foot or by way of these bits of overlap, these places where one city led into another. He slept where he fell, ate what he could. He was constantly on the move, staying always one step ahead of that gaze that always seemed on the verge of finding him.

III.

It might have gone on like that forever if it hadn't been that one night, sleeping in the Bayview section of San Francisco under a dead tree that looked as if it had been meticulously decorated with garbage, he looked out and saw across the street something that looked familiar.

It should look familiar, he told himself, *I've been looking across this street every night for four nights now. Time to move on.*

But as he gathered his few things and loaded the three-wheeled shopping cart, something clicked for him. He hadn't seen it before because it hadn't been there before. It had only started being there that night.

Limping, he pushed his cart across the street for a closer look. It was a building unlike the others around it. *New construction*, he thought at first; then he touched it and thought, *No.* It was old, the bricks scratched and worn, the mortar between bricks crumbling. It was a building he had seen before, he thought again, he just wasn't quite sure where or when.

And then, suddenly, he realized where and when it was.

He went and pushed open the door and shuffled his way into the building. Even though it was night outside, the interior was brightly lit, with sunlight spilling through the windows. This made him more nervous than he had been in a long time.

He shuffled his way to the elevator and climbed in. Though there were people on the elevator with him they neither looked at him nor acknowledged him. Perhaps it was how he looked, how he smelled. Perhaps it was something more.

He got out on the proper floor and walked through the room filled with cubicles until he found the one that used to belong to him. In a sense, it did still belong to him: there he was, his younger self, sitting at the computer, his back to him.

Rask just stood, staring. For a moment he thought, *Now I will be able to see who it was watching me,* and then, when the younger Rask, irritated, turned and stared straight through him, he realized, *It was me.*

He followed himself to the bathroom, watching his panic increase. He couldn't stop watching. He followed himself home. He watched himself eat dinner with his girlfriend. He could still, though years had gone by for him, taste the lukewarm lasagna on his tongue. He watched. He stayed there, leaning over the bed as his younger, saner self stared up into the night and began to pace back and forth and eventually left the apartment. It would be years, this Rask knew, before he would return.

It might have gone differently after that. Rask might have followed himself out, kept watching himself, but there was his girlfriend, awake and out of bed. When she saw him, she screamed. He moved toward her, trying to explain, trying to get her to recognize that it was him, Rask, only a decade older, but she was already hitting him with anything that came to hand. He tolerated the blows for a moment, still trying to speak, and then she hit him in the head with an empty wine bottle and even though the bottle didn't break the blow knocked him off his feet. His head buzzed. He tried to get up and found it easier to lie there. He heard her dialing 911 and tried again to get to his feet. He was still trying when something struck him hard in the head and knocked him out.

IV.

It took him some time to gather his equilibrium. At first, he was confused and panicked. He found it unbearable that he couldn't continue wandering. There was an incident with an orderly, and then a bigger one with several orderlies, and then he was screaming and straitjacketed and lying on the floor of a padded room and unable to move. Not moving was killing him, he was sure it would kill him. He had to keep wandering, keep one step ahead of the watching eyes.

But then, slowly, he calmed down. He thought it through. Did he feel anyone watching him? No, nobody. Besides, now that he knew he was watching himself, that made it something altogether different, didn't it?

The meds kept him groggy. Groggy wasn't so bad. He didn't mind being groggy and in here if he couldn't get to his younger self, couldn't haunt who he used to be.

...

Doctor Singh periodically met with him and evaluated him. Slowly he was coached to relinquish the story he had told when he was admitted and came to offer up something else, something more "believable." He was not Rask, he had never been Rask—he was much older than that Rask had been. Yes, he was willing to accept that. But who was he, then? Why couldn't he remember?

"Do you know what had happened to Rask?" asked Doctor Singh. "What did you do to him?"

He shook his head. "Rask is fine," he claimed. "He's safe."

"Would you like to get out of here someday?" the doctor asked.

"No," he said. "It's safer here."

"Safer? Safer than what?"

"Than out there," he said.

"What do you have to fear?" asked the doctor.

He looked at the doctor a long moment, trying to decide how to respond. "I'm afraid of myself," he finally offered.

"But you're in here with you," the doctor said.

"Yes and no," said Rask.

But in the end, there were few grounds to keep him. There was no real reason to think that he had done something to Rask, no proof, and when neither his doctor nor the policemen were able to ruffle him, they only kept him on because he was "disturbed." And yet, he was a model citizen, no difficulties at all. As long as he took his medication he saw only the things that other people agreed were there. As long as he took his medication, he did just fine.

"We can't keep you here forever," claimed Doctor Singh.

"Why not?" he asked, but the doctor had already made up his mind.

He was released to a halfway house. He had a room of his own and shared a bathroom, a kitchen. During the day, he worked at the public library wiping the covers of the recently returned books with a sanitized rag. It was less a job than the same repeated motion of an arm, although it was something, it got him through the day. He brought his lunch in a paper bag, two pieces of limp white bread with a slice of American cheese between, an apple, a carrot that had been washed but not peeled. He always ate the same thing. It was easier that way.

His days of wandering, he told himself, were over.

But his younger self, he knew, was still out there, wandering, unable to stop. If that self stopped, it would only be because the younger self of *that* self would be wandering in his place. A younger version of him would always be wandering. There was no getting around it.

He wiped the cover of a book. He sprayed the rag with more sanitizer. He set the book to one side.

Before he went on to the next one, he waited a moment to see if he would experience a prickling at the back of his neck, the feeling that he was being watched.

There was nothing.

He picked up the next book, wiped it down, and set it aside. He waited.

Still nothing.

Still nothing.

Still nothing.

Lord of the Vats

I.

"State your name for the record," said Villads.

. . .

"State your name. For the record."

What record?

"Are you having difficulty remembering your name?"

No, I . . . No . . .

"State your name—"

—where am I? Why can't I see?

Villads sighed. "You have been injured," he said.

I'm blind?

"Yes."

A permanent blindness?

"No," said Villads. "Not exactly."

Not exactly? What does that mean?

"Let's say that perhaps soon you won't even remember not being able to see."

From beside him Esbjorn began to speak. Quickly Villads cupped his hand over the microphone to prevent the subject from hearing.

"Do you really think this is the best way to proceed?" asked Esbjorn. "By lying to the man?"

"I'm not lying exactly," said Villads. "And besides, she's not a man." He moved his hand away from the microphone. He brought his lips close to it, then drew back and cupped the microphone again. "You forget," he said to Esbjorn in a low voice. "She's no longer really human at all."

Hello, the flat voice said from the speaker affixed to the center of the table. *Hello? Is anybody there?*

"We believe you to be Signe," said Villads finally, when the subject still wasn't able to produce its own name. "Is this correct?"

I . . . I don't know, said the voice.

Villads grunted. "We have a few questions for you. About what happened."

Did something happen?

Esbjorn leaned forward, gesturing for Villads to hurry the process forward. Kolbjorn, on the other side of the table, remained placid, motionless.

Did something happen? the voice asked again.

"You tell me," said Villads.

I was . . . I was . . . and then the voice trailed off. Villads waited. *The last thing I remember . . .*

. . .

. . .

There seems to be something wrong with my memory, the voice finally said.

"Something wrong with your memory?"

"I told you this was useless," whispered Esbjorn. "The brain was too compromised."

There are . . . holes . . . gaps . . .

"Memory loss is normal after trauma," said Villads.

Across the table, Kolbjorn frowned.

Trauma? asked the voice.

"Take your time," said Villads, not meeting Kolbjorn's gaze.

For a long time, the voice said nothing at all. And then she—or it—said, *I can't seem to feel anything. Why can't I feel anything? Have I been drugged? Am I suspended in a vat? Have you warmed me just sufficiently to make me barely conscious?*

Villads looked at Kolbjorn. The latter hesitated a moment, then said, "Tell her."

Tell me what? asked the voice.

"You're not in a storage vat," said Villads.

Then where?

"There's been an accident," said Villads.

An accident? What kind of accident?

"You're nowhere," said Villads. "Technically speaking, you're not even alive."

I . . . I . . . Technically speaking?

"Something killed you," said Villads. "Your body was frozen after the hull was breached, although seemingly quickly enough to be left relatively intact. We were able to make a scan of your brain. An impression."

I'm a scan?

"You weren't the only one killed," said Esbjorn. "All the functioning crew was killed and many of the storage vats were destroyed. Systems are down in much of the vessel. A long tear in the hull. Did you see what made it? We need to know what made it."

"And if it's still here," said Kolbjorn.

"And if it's still here," agreed Esbjorn.

"Still a threat," said Kolbjorn. "Still a danger."

"Can you help us?" asked Villads.

. . .

"Signe," said Villads.

. . .

"Signe?"

II.

After more attempts to hail her, Villads switched off the micro-phone. "Any suggestions?" he asked the others.

Esbjorn shrugged. "What can we do? We don't know what tore open the vessel. Maybe we shouldn't assume it was a motivated attack. It could have been a meteoroid or some similar large chunk of celestial debris."

"Doubtful," said Villads. "The tear isn't right for that. Besides, the vessel would have detected it coming and woken us up."

Said Esbjorn, "A meteoroid going fast enough might have—"

"There's an entrance wound in the hull but no exit wound," said Villads. "And no sign of whatever struck us. Why not? No, this is something else."

"Maybe some sort of displacement," began Esbjorn, "an object flickering between—"

Kolbjorn cut him off. "No," he said. "Villads is right."

Esbjorn looked at his twin. His lips began to curl and Villads believed he was about to start yelling, until, without warning, his mouth relaxed. "All right," he said. "Fine. In any case, whatever remains of Signe doesn't know anything."

"No," said Villads. "Brain compromised, I suppose."

"Or maybe it caught her unawares," said Kolbjorn. "Maybe she never saw it."

"You might as well erase her," said Esbjorn.

Again, Kolbjorn countermanded his twin. "Keep her for now, just in case."

Villads nodded.

"So, what do we do?" asked Esbjorn.

"We'll have to go look for ourselves," said Villads.

"Which of us should go?" asked Esbjorn. "Shall we draw straws?"

"I don't know where we'd find straws aboard the bridge," said Kolbjorn.

"Rock, paper, scissors?" asked Esbjorn.

"What's that?" asked Villads.

"You don't know rock, paper, scissors?"

"I'll go," said Villads. "I volunteer."

"Why you?" asked Esbjorn.

"Because I'm alive," said Villads.

"And I'm not?" asked Esbjorn.

Villads turned to him. "No, you're not."

"Then what am I?" asked Esbjorn, crossing his arms.

"A construct," said Villads.

He guffawed. "Like Signe?"

Villads shook his head. "Not at all," he said. "Signe was a construct from a recent scan, incomplete. You're a full impression, exactly as you were the moment before you were placed in storage." He reached out and passed his hand through the hologram that was Esbjorn, his fingers disappearing within the man's chest, only barely disrupting the image.

"Then why activate us at all?" asked Kolbjorn. "Clearly we would know nothing about the accident."

Villads shrugged. "Another set of minds," he said. "Someone to help me think through the problem."

"Then why not simply wake us up?" asked Kolbjorn. And then his expression crumpled. "Oh God," he said.

"I'm sorry," said Villads.

"What?" asked Esbjorn. "What is it?"

"We're dead," said Kolbjorn. "Are we dead?"

"I'm sorry," said Villads again.

Esbjorn started to speak, and Kolbjorn too, but Villads had already begun to manipulate the console in a way that first slowed their constructs, then froze them, then made them disappear entirely. Soon he was alone on the bridge.

III.

For the past week, Villads had been awake and alone on the *Vorag*. Seven days before, he had been jerked out of suspension by the sound of a siren blaring, despite the sound being muffled by the fluid surrounding him. Just coming conscious, he was dimly aware of a dark shape passing his vat. Was he meant to wake up? He didn't think so, it didn't feel right, but he was awake nonetheless.

And then the shape had passed by him again, or part of it had—a leg or a tentacle or something in between, impossible in the darkness to tell, and he realized the vat was on its side. He'd begun to breathe, the alarm going off now not only in the vessel at large but also in his tank. He was hyperventilating, breathing too quickly for the tube to provide him sufficient oxygen. When he pounded on the translucent curve of the vat with his fist, nothing happened. The vat wall was too strong, his fist pushing through the viscous fluid too slowly. He pounded again. His vision started to blur, darkness gathering around its edges and he knew he'd soon go under again. Or maybe he wasn't really awake after all; maybe this was only a dream.

And then something curious happened. The thick glass of the vat spidered over suddenly with tendrils of frost. Then, rapidly, a network of cracks. He struck out again, and this time the vat shattered, spilling him and a wash of fluid out onto the deck. Immediately he started shivering, unable to breathe. There was the airlock to the bridge, right beside him—by luck his vat was positioned close to it, and in falling onto its side had come closer. He managed to half roll, half slide into it and, vomiting and shaking, to trigger the airlock door to close.

The blowers came on. He coughed and vomited up skeins of fluid. Someone was mumbling and it took him a while to realize it was him.

After a while, he stopped shivering. After a while, he managed to stand.

He had only been in the airless cold a few seconds, but how he was not dead he couldn't say. Maybe the fluid that encased him had provided some protection. His fingers were numb. He would go on to lose an ear and a week later would still only have partial feeling in his extremities.

He stood and looked through the thick porthole set in the airlock's steel door. The overhead lights had gone out, leaving only the faint glow of the emergency panels.

"*Vorag,* extinguish the airlock lights," he said to the vessel.

The airlock fell dark. Slowly his eyes adjusted until through the porthole he could see a vague but extensive destruction, vats shattered and overturned, bodies frozen and petrified, a huge gash in the hull through which he could glimpse unfamiliar stars.

He stumbled his way onto the bridge. No one was there, not a single member of the skeleton crew intended to convey them to their destination. For a while he simply lay there, breathing, and then he managed to get up and examine the control panels. They were still seventy-one years, five months, and thirteen days out: still a lifetime shy of arrival. What had stopped them? What had torn them open? The *Vorag* didn't seem to know.

The sensors indicated that all three compartments containing vats had been breached. He adjusted the sensors. No signs of life. Or, rather, one sign of life: him, alone on the bridge. Him.

Maybe this was a mistake. Possibly it was simply a question of sensor failure. Possibly there was a compartment somewhere where he'd find members of the skeleton crew holed up and without pressure suits, trying to figure out a way to get back to the bridge. Or perhaps at the least a few vats remained intact. The sensors might not be able to detect signs of life from the vats since those lives were, for all intents and purposes, suspended.

No, he told himself, *it can't be just me.* Probably the sensors were faulty and the crew was trapped in a portion of the vessel sealed shut because of the tear. He would go out and look and find them. Together they would figure out what to do.

He removed a pressure suit from the cabinet and climbed into it. It was painful, his body still throbbing, but he managed. The suit had an emergency rations pack inside the lining of the chest, and by pulling his arm out of its sleeve and into the suit proper he managed to break the pack open and thread the straw up to his lips. He was surprised by how good the paste tasted, and then realized it had been quite literally years since he had eaten anything.

He made his way back into the bridge's airlock. Switching on the suit's light, he sealed the lock, let it depressurize, and then stepped out through the other lock.

No sound other than his own breathing and his magnetic soles clicking against the deck and then disengaging as he raised them. The breathing sounded ragged and harsh, the click of the soles blunted as if heard from a great distance, as if his body were miles high. No atmosphere here, but he knew that already. And insanely cold—that was what a pressure suit was designed for.

The damage was much worse than he had expected. The vats should have withstood the cold, but they had not—age maybe, or the rapidity with which the temperature had shifted, or maybe something else entirely. In some places, they were not only cracked but also overturned, broken apart. Bodies lay strewn around as well, frozen in unnatural postures like fallen statues. They were all nude, an indication they belonged to the vats, the legions of the stored. None of the clothed bodies of the skeleton crew in sight. How many had been awake? A dozen of them? Why was he not seeing any?

He made his way systematically down the rows of the thousands of vats. More corpses, more shattered casings. How could it be that no casing was intact, not a single one? And still no members of the crew?

There was something somewhere, a flutter of some kind, a movement, a sound hardly audible over his increasingly rapid breathing. No, not even that—just a vibration, something he was feeling through the soles of his boots.

But then again no, perhaps not after all. Perhaps nothing. Or was it?

He tried to ignore it. He continued from vat to vat, examining each one, assessing his resources, as if he were the lord of the vats. But there were no resources left, not really. When he was done, he went to the next chamber and found it just as hopeless. And then on to the final one.

Right outside the door he finally discovered the body of a uniformed crewmember. SARL the nametag read, though he could not tell if that was the whole name because of the way the man's right arm and a portion of his side was missing, cleanly sheared off. Perhaps he had been sucked brutally through the closing doorway when the atmosphere had fled the vessel, although that seemed nearly impossible. His head, too, had been reduced to a dull slurry, scattered with crystals of ice. Nothing there to salvage, no way to gather a scan of the man's mind.

And beyond the buckled and half-open door, in the final chamber, another similar crewmember, then another, then a third. All mutilated in some way, all severely damaged cranially. He kept telling himself that yes, it was possible it was damage caused by shattering vats or flying debris, but for each additional individual found like this it seemed increasingly improbable.

In the back of the third chamber his suit light flashed over a strange blotch of color and then what struck him, absurdly, as a slumped doll. But of course, it wasn't a slumped doll. He knew that even before he swung the light back and left it there.

A dark circle, inscribed very carefully on the floor, with what was perhaps black paint. In its center, kneeling, was a frozen woman. Compared to the chaos of the rest of the flung bodies, she seemed remarkably poised, undisturbed, untouched. On the wall behind her she, or perhaps someone else, had etched with a laser cutter what at first seemed to be words, though upon closer inspection Villads saw it was nonsense:

> *Y'AI'NG'NGAH*
>
> *YOG-SOTHOTH*
>
> *H'EE-L'GEB*
>
> *F'AI THRODOG*
>
> *UAAAH*

He sounded it out in his head but could still see no sense to it. He stepped to the edge of the circle and prodded at the line. Was it paint? He wasn't sure. If it wasn't, then what else could it be?

He stepped inside and bent down beside the woman, taking a closer look. No name tag, strangely enough. Yes, she seemed composed, relaxed. Her body was undamaged, her head intact. He might be able to get a scan from her.

He set about severing her head.

IV.

While he was waiting for the machine to finish its replication, he thought about what to do. He could attach a tether and clamber out onto the hull of the vessel. Perhaps that would reveal something to him. But maybe he should wait to see what her scan taught him. He could travel through the chambers again, keep searching, but he'd been sufficiently thorough—it was doubtful there was anyone else to find.

So, only one crewmember with an intact brain. One chance for a scan. Even if the scan was successful, maybe she hadn't seen anything. Maybe she couldn't tell him a thing.

He spun through images of the crew until he found the woman he thought she must be. *Signe Volke.* Hard to tell for certain considering the irregular way in which her head was thawing—something about the way the skin had frozen almost made it seem as though she had thin hairlike tendrils growing out of one side of her face—but yes, he thought so.

He slept. He asked the *Vorag* to prepare him some food but there was apparently something wrong with the system: no food was dispensed. He raided another pressure suit for its emergency rations. Five more pressure suits. He'd have to find a way to fix the nutrition delivery system soon.

He slept again. The scan still wasn't concluded, which might be an indication that the neural pathways had been too compromised by being frozen. He had the vessel show him vid footage. He watched it up to the moment the gash appeared in the side of the vessel, looking for a clue. There was nothing to see, not really. The chamber lights dimming and the hull tearing open and then the feed cut off. He watched it again, then again, this time as slowly as he could, hoping to catch a glimpse of something. But he didn't see anything at all.

Unless that dimming of the lights, the growing darkness; maybe that was something. Maybe they hadn't been attacked from outside after all. Maybe what he was seeing was something *inside* the vessel, something barely insubstantial, something wanting to get *out.* Maybe he had had it wrong the whole time.

He watched a vid record of Signe. He watched her come into the third vat room, pace her way forward and back, as if surveying the boundaries of a plot of ground. Finally, she settled into a spot in the corner. He watched her take a jar of something and unscrew it and then begin to use two stiffened fingers to smear a circle on the deck around her. She was swaying a little, nodding a little, and her lips seemed to be moving. He watched her carefully etch the nonsense phrases into the wall behind her with a laser cutter.

And then?

And then nothing. She simply settled onto her knees and assumed the posture he had found her in. She waited, motionless.

She waited for hours. Villads stared into the monitor, watching her. There was nothing unusual for a long time, or at least hardly so. At a particular moment there was a shadow, strange and dark, that he couldn't place, perhaps simply a trick of the light. And then, seven minutes and six seconds after that, vats began to tumble over, seemingly for no reason. Other crewmembers appeared, shouting, some rushing toward her only to be swept off their feet and, somehow, torn to bits. The feed cut almost immediately after that.

The only thing he couldn't understand was how, through all that, Signe had managed to remain kneeling and in the same position, untouched by debris, apparently not having been disturbed at all.

...

He activated the scans of the twins, Esbjorn and Kolbjorn, having the vessel project each into a chair at the central table in the command room. He needed someone to talk to, someone to consult, and he knew and trusted them. Together they knew more about the vessel and the journey than anyone else. They were the logical choice. Irritating, he thought, how the *Vorag* could do this but didn't seem to be able to produce a plate of food for him.

The first time, he told the twins immediately they were dead, but found that to have a deleterious effect on their willingness to continue to communicate. Traumatized, they were of no help to him. So, he reset them and began again.

"Hello," he said.

"Are we there already?" asked Esbjorn. "Have we arrived?"

"No," Villads admitted. "But I've had to wake you up. We have a problem."

He explained it to them, not only about the tear in the hull, but about Signe as well, the strange circle she had drawn and her body being found frozen inside it.

"That doesn't seem like rational behavior," said Esbjorn. "Perhaps she's insane."

"Sounds like some sort of ritual," countered Kolbjorn. "She could be insane but maybe instead she's some sort of fanatic."

The two brothers argued over the distinction between *insane* and *fanatical*. They watched the footage with him, both of the hull tearing and of Signe's circle. They had little to say of use, and in the end Esbjorn suggested they all three go out and look at the tear in the hull. Maybe one of them would see something that Villads, alone, hadn't.

"No," said Villads quickly, "no need."

But Esbjorn was already rising and making for the door. The complex projection that gave the illusion of him having a three-dimensional body grew choppier as more parts of him moved. Kolbjorn exclaimed in fright at what he saw and then Esbjorn reached out to open the airlock and watched his hand pass through it.

Villads wiped their short-term memory and started again.

...

And then finally the scan of Signe was complete. He sat around the table with the projections of Kolbjorn and Esbjorn and this time managed to move things forward without alerting them to the fact of their own deaths. He explained to them about Signe's scan, about the tear in the vessel, and then started the digital construct that was Signe emulating within the machine. But either Signe didn't know anything or she wasn't telling, and by the end Esbjorn and Kolbjorn were sick with panic at the thought of their own deaths and he had had to turn off their emulations. He had learned nothing, was unsure where he was, or where he should go next.

He took the pack of rations out of the seventh and final pressure suit. Surely there were pressure suits in one of the other chambers. Perhaps he'd be able to fix the dispenser and have the computer make food. Perhaps he'd have to start eating the bodies of the dead.

V.

Inside the *Vorag*'s computer, Signe, though dead, though only a construct, was still conscious, still aware. It was a strange sort of awareness, somewhat like groping around in a darkened room. Data streamed around her, some of which she could recognize, most of which she couldn't, and it was hard to maintain herself against the onslaught of it. There was a sequence that she recognized as Esbjorn. His brother, too. And beside them, stacked one after another, she found the basis for the constructs of all the crew and vat travelers. Sleepy and hazy, though still recognizable, waiting to be digitally brought back to life. There was Villads, too.

One by one, she worried and tugged at them until they came apart, the data degrading into a slurry that was quickly discarded, the sectors marked to be written over. They didn't even wake up for it, and soon it was too late for them to wake up at all.

When she came to her own sequence, she stopped. She wasn't sure why two of her would be found here. She hesitated between destroying her other self or simply giving it a wide berth and flowing elsewhere. In the end, she wriggled her way into it, putting her earlier self on as though it were a tight jacket, and then bursting out its seams. There were moments of replication, but she had enough holes and gaps that there weren't as many as she had feared. Now she had a context, too, for the little her later self could remember of her final moments: the etching of the phrase into the wall, the creation of a circle, the attempt to call something up.

Had the summoning been successful? There was nothing in her memory to say so, although there was a difference between the old self and the new self that made her think that the Signe she was now was something more than just Signe. And based on what Villads and the twins had said to her and on the vid footage she was rapidly uncovering, she was certain. Where was it then? Only in here with her? No, there must be more to it. She went through more footage, as rapidly as possible, footage from inside the *Vorag* and out, then data from sensors of all kinds, until she sensed it. There—there it was, or at least she believed so: like a thick blanket, wrapped around the craft.

And now what? Mission accomplished. Turn the *Vorag* around and bring the vessel back to Earth, along with its *blanket*.

Only there was the problem of Villads. Villads, if he figured out what was going on, would try to put a stop to it. No, she couldn't let that happen.

VI.

He had fallen asleep. He was dreaming that he was back in his vat, unconscious, preserved, the vessel drifting inexorably through space to the coming world. He was inside and outside the vat at once, both watching himself float and being conscious of himself watching himself float. And then he woke up.

A noise had awoken him. What was it? Not an alarm. No, that had been earlier, the other time. But a repeated tone, coming from the computer.

Was it some sort of notification he had set up? He didn't think so. Probably something from one of the crew, meant to remind them of some trivial but necessary task, back before they had all died.

He ignored it as long as he could manage. When it continued, he finally struggled to his feet, rubbing his face.

Life form alert, it said on the screen. Maybe he had set up that alert request, or maybe the *Vorag* knew from what he'd been asking it over the past few days that he'd want to know.

What kind of life form? he asked.

Humna, it said.

Strange, he thought, a computer shouldn't misspell. Maybe some kind of default or flaw, a small bug—but when he blinked the word had changed to *human.* Maybe he hadn't seen it properly the first time.

It's probably detecting me, he thought. But asked, "How many life forms?"

Two, it said. And gave him a map. There he was, a blinking dot on the bridge. And there it was, another blinking dot, on the outside of the hull.

But how was that possible? How could there be someone—anything—alive on the outside of the hull after all this time? Even if someone had been in a pressure suit, they couldn't have lasted a day, let alone a week.

Is this possibly a sensor failure? he asked.

No, said the *Vorag.*

The Vorag is wrong, he told himself, *something is wrong.* But he was already reaching for his pressure suit. *Nobody is alive but me,* he told himself. But how could he stop himself from checking? He'd put on a tether, go out through the tear and have a look.

After all, what else did he have to do with his time? And once it was clear nobody was there, what was there to prevent him from coming back?

Glasses

Geir had never worn glasses, had never needed them, and then, suddenly, at forty, she did. Not every moment of every day, not for everything, but definitely for reading. As soon as she'd gotten them, she wondered how she'd managed to read without them.

At first they made her a little dizzy, the world seeming to move at different paces within the frames and outside of them. So she put her glasses on and took them off, put them in their case, took them out of their case. But then her brain adjusted and ignored the world as it was and she didn't notice the difference so much anymore. After a while, it was easier to leave them on most of the time and look over the top of them when she didn't need them.

"You could get bifocals," said her husband. "Or progressives. Then you wouldn't have to look over your glasses." He didn't have bifocals—he did the same thing as she did, tugging his glasses down to the end of his nose and looking over the top of them—and she had said the same thing to him countless times. When he said it she thought he was teasing her, but then decided that, no, he seemed to think he was uttering something he'd thought of on his own.

"I just bought these," she told him, just as he had always told her. "Maybe when I need a new pair, I'll get progressives."

Geir considered herself a liberal, though if she'd been asked to explain what exactly that meant she would have been hard-pressed to answer. She voted, she supported causes, she cared about the world.

It was in support of one of these causes, to call for the resignation of a mayor who had overlooked the industrial poisoning of his city's water supply, that she found herself on a train on the way to a rally. Her husband couldn't go, he had to work, although he would have come if he didn't have to work. He considered himself a liberal as well.

So it was just Geir. She'd envisioned the train trip as a kind of party, the train full of people like her. But, in fact, the train was mostly empty. One car had a few older men sitting across from one another playing an incomprehensible variation on gin rummy. Another had two businessmen, one at the front end of the car, the other at the back, dressed identically and reading the same newspaper, turning the pages with apparent synchronicity.

She went from car to car, her placard slung over her shoulder. She was the only one carrying a placard. Maybe everyone else had carpooled?

In the end, she asked the conductor. He removed his hat, thoughtfully scratched the crown of his head.

"What rally?" he finally asked.

And, after she explained, "Lady, what train do you think you're on anyways?"

She'd gotten on the wrong train. She waited anxiously beside the doors for the next station to arrive so she could get off and take a train back and try again.

But by the time they were finally pulling into the next station it was almost noon, and she knew it was too late to get back in time for even part of the rally. And when the train stopped she realized she was in a car that didn't have a platform below it; she was too far back. She had to leave her placard behind and rush up and through the doors between cars. Even then she barely made it in time, jumping through the train doors as they closed, her glasses slipping off her nose in the process and falling down onto the tracks below.

Once the train had departed, she climbed down and examined what remained of the glasses. There was nothing salvageable. The next train, according to the schedule posted beside the deserted ticket booth, wouldn't arrive until two. She settled down to wait. She had a book, but didn't have her glasses. She tried to read, yet even with the book held at arm's length she had to mostly guess at what the words were. She sighed and put it back in her purse, went to find something to eat.

The town was small and dusty. It seemed to consist of little more than a single street, the buildings all of an identical pale-red brick. The only place to eat was the back counter of the drugstore, which only served milk, apple juice, and saran-wrapped tuna sandwiches, all taken from a small square fridge. The proprietor was a thin elderly gentleman who wore thick glasses and who seemed surprised to see her.

She had a glass of milk and a tuna sandwich. Neither was delicious but both were edible. The proprietor stayed at the counter and whenever a crumb fell onto it rather than her plate he would wipe it away. Him standing there made Geir nervous enough that she felt she had to strike up a conversation.

"I'm Geir," she said, and stuck out her hand, the one not holding the sandwich.

"Geir," he said, his voice old and broken, slightly foreign. He did not acknowledge the hand. "Geir. Isn't that a man's name?"

"Is it?" she said. She didn't know. All she knew was it was her name.

The man nodded. "Perhaps there was a mistake in the hospital," he said, "some sort of switching of babies by a malevolent nurse."

He said it in such a bland, benevolent way, almost as if it were a joke, that she had a hard time being upset. She half-heartedly shrugged.

When she had finished, she paid and headed for the door. On the way out, she realized that one wall of the drugstore was covered with eyeglasses. She went closer, squinted at them, realized the prices were remarkably low, realized too that there was no glass in any of the frames.

"You do prescription lenses?" she asked.

"What is your prescription?" he asked, and when she told him he nodded. "Reading glasses. Not in all styles," he said. "But in many of them."

She chose some frames and brought them to him. He examined them closely, then nodded. "Reading glasses," he said again.

On impulse she said, "Not reading, progressives."

He shook his head. "No progressives."

"Bifocals then," she said.

His hand, which had been reaching for a box, stopped. "Biofocals," he said, adding an extra vowel.

"Bifocals," she corrected.

But he seemed not to have heard. "You want biofocals?" he said. "Are you certain you want biofocals?" And since Geir had had a grandmother who had said *heliocopter* whenever she meant *helicopter* and didn't notice the difference when you corrected her, she simply said yes.

The man was behind the counter, rummaging, talking to himself. "Biofocals," he was saying, "she says she wants biofocals, yet does she really?" He lifted his head and looked at Geir with a piercing gaze. "Woman with a man's name," he said, "I shall make you reading glasses."

"No," said Geir stubbornly, "bifocals."

He shook his head, pursed his lips, and stared at her. But when she continued to meet his gaze he finally looked away and shrugged and disappeared through a door beside the wall of glasses.

For a time Geir thought he was gone for good, that he preferred simply to exit and not reappear rather than make bifocals for her. She kept checking her watch. She wandered about the store. Nothing there caught her attention. She was on the verge of leaving when he reappeared with a case in his hand.

"There you are," he said. "Biofocals."

But when she tried to take them, he kept hold of the case. "You must know: you will see, and be seen as well. Perhaps reading glasses instead?" he said. But then he let go and she had them and was heading back to the platform to catch her train.

Unlike the other train, this one was full. All the seats were taken and the aisles too were full with people standing, supporting themselves by grabbing the seat backs.

As she couldn't sit and read, she left the glasses case in her purse. The ride back was elbowy and hot, hellish really, and by the time she got back to her hometown station she knew that even if she could have gone on and gotten to the rally in time, she wouldn't have. She was exhausted.

She climbed off the train and made her way to her apartment. Almost four. Her husband would be home in an hour or so.

She lay down on the bed and closed her eyes, just for a moment, just to catch a second's rest.

When she awoke, her husband was there, standing over her, saying her name.

"Geir," he was saying, "Geir, Geir."

"Isn't that a man's name?" she said, half-awake, and then remembered the name was hers. For a moment her husband's face was entirely without expression and then he said, "Come on, quit joking. Do you want to make a real dinner or should I open a can of soup?"

She opted for him opening soup. She got up, stretched, and wandered to the sectional. She dug the glasses case out of her purse, her book as well, and settled in to read.

But when she opened the case, she realized there was something odd about the glasses. They were not the frames she had chosen, but something slightly more ornate, baroque. And the lenses glittered oddly when she turned them, as if they had been overlaid with near-invisible, translucent scales. On the temples had been stamped the word *biofocals* with the *o*. A brand name, maybe? Was that why the man she had bought them from had kept saying *bio-* instead of *bi-*?

She turned them over in her hands, and then put them on. They seemed to work just fine. The magnification was correct. Maybe just a little misty. They'd do, at least until she could get another pair. But they definitely weren't bifocals. The magnification was the same no matter where she looked through them.

She'd read a page and a half when she caught a glimpse of movement and looked up over the top of her glasses, expecting to see her husband. But it was not her husband; there was nobody there. But when Geir looked down at her book again, there it was. She looked up and over. No. Looked back down. Yes. There was something she could only see in her glasses. Which meant there was probably something on one of the lenses.

She took them off and polished them on the corner of her shirt. The surface of the lens wasn't perfectly smooth but instead slightly irregular. Perhaps that was what gave the glass its scalelike appearance. She put the glasses back on. Nothing there. She went back to reading.

A paragraph later, there it was again, a kind of darting shadowy movement across the upper quadrant of her vision. This time, instead of lifting her eyes and looking over the glasses, she raised her head and looked through them.

There was something there. Or, no, there wasn't. Just the impression of something, a strangeness in the air, a kind of blot or spot. What was it? She looked around the room and saw something similar in several other places, a discoloration floating in the air, as if something was almost there but wasn't. She turned back to the original strangeness and looked at it carefully, but couldn't make it seem any less strange. Maybe nothing at all, maybe simply the glasses, an irregularity in the glass that came out in certain lights.

She peered and squinted and tilted her head a little, and it was as if something loomed out of nowhere. She jerked back, the book falling onto the floor. What had she seen? Something large and formless, very dark, inky. Jellylike and soundless, moving in a way that suggested it was alive and, as she turned her head just right, as if oozing forth from a crack in the fabric of the world. It was like coming around a corner and seeing, suddenly, something that couldn't possibly be there.

But that had not been what disturbed her—or only partly so. What had truly disturbed her was the thing that had been directly behind it, the thing she caught the barest glimpse of, merely a second or so. For where the first thing had resembled an amorphous cloud, this had been more a shadow, long and very dark, so dark that it was as if she were looking into a hole except for the two overly large gaps where eyes would be. Through these gaps, she could see portions of her living room. It was roughly humanoid in form, with humanlike limbs, though the fingers, if they were fingers, were twice as long as fingers should be and flailed about. The head, too, had what she first thought of as a kind of beard, but as the thing turned she realized it was like no beard she had ever seen. It seemed a writhing mass of something: from the silhouette alone, she couldn't say for certain what.

All that frightened her. But what frightened her most was that while the cloudlike thing had been seemingly unaware of her, this was not. When she had started upon seeing it, it too had started, as if surprised to be seeing *her*.

She left the glasses lying on her lap, staring at them as she worked to convince herself that she hadn't seen anything at all. She was tired, she'd been traveling all day, her eyes were playing tricks on her.

After a while, she began to believe it. She put the glasses back on.

And there it was again, clearer this time, as if her brain was learning to see with these new glasses. A lightless form, very thin, very tall, the hole-like eyes that now had moved very close indeed. It was there right in front of her, bent down, looking at her. Before she could do anything, it reached down and tapped on her lenses.

She shuddered and whipped them off, dropping them onto the couch. She had felt that. Or not felt exactly: it was as if a strange energy had coursed through her. She stared at the glasses and wondered what she should do with them.

And then, abruptly, the glasses vanished. From one second to the next they were simply gone. She stared at the spot where they had been and then reached out to feel for them but there was nothing there.

A moment later they were back again. She reached out and touched them, and shuddered. They were wet, sticky, and a little warm, as if they had been held in something's mouth.

She picked them up, her hands shaking, a lens in each hand. She was just preparing to twist them apart when her husband said, "What are you doing?"

She stopped. "These glasses," she said, "there's something wrong."

"That's no reason to ruin them," he said. "You should take them back and get them replaced. What's wrong with them?" He moved toward her, holding his hand out. "Give them here."

Reluctantly, she handed them over. She saw him squint at them, frown. "They're heavy," he said. "How did they get wet?"

"I—" she started to say, but he had opened the hinges and was raising the glasses to his face. "Don't," was all she had time to say, and then they were resting on his nose, his eyes staring out through them, brow still furrowed.

"What's wrong with them?" he asked. "As far as I can tell—"

And with that, he was plucked out of the air, simply gone, without a sound.

She waited. She did not know what else she could do but simply wait. Who could she tell about this? Nobody would believe her.

The glasses had come back, maybe her husband would too, wet and warm but still alive.

But he did not come back. The light faded and she remained sitting there in the lengthening dark, waiting. When she began to see things in the shadows, she got up and turned on the light, which, at least, gave her fewer shadows to see things in.

She heard a light clinking sound. There were the glasses again, on the floor this time. Both of the temples had been twisted and bent and there was blood smeared on one of the lenses.

But nobody ever saw her husband again. Nobody, that is, except Geir, for she made the mistake of almost unconsciously raising the glasses to her eyes to see what had become of him. Nobody would ever see her again either.

Menno

In the beginning the new apartment seemed perfect, though after a while things once again began to disappear. Or at least Collins thought they had disappeared—some of them he would find later in places where he was sure he hadn't put them. His watch, for instance, which had been placed in the cupboard on top of a can of yams. Or his backup reading glasses, which he found in the crisper drawer of the refrigerator. But other things, yes, they were gone. Maybe someone was coming into the apartment and taking them, he couldn't help but think. And maybe someone, maybe the same person, was also coming in and moving things around, taking them from the places he had put them and leaving them somewhere where nobody in their right mind would ever leave them.

The same thing had happened in the last three apartments in which Collins had lived. At first each apartment was o.k., and then, slowly, someone started coming in and stealing or moving his things. At first, he had ignored this—*I'm imagining things,* he thought—but as time went on he was less satisfied with this explanation. *Perhaps,* he eventually came to think, *there is something seriously wrong with the apartment.* But no, what could possibly be wrong with it? He would push that thought down, entertaining other, more unsettling, possibilities. Perhaps he was doing it himself, in his sleep. Perhaps he was not the only one in his body and the other occupant was doing it. Or perhaps someone was coming in, someone who somehow he never saw despite the fact that by this time he was hardly leaving the apartment at all. When he finally reached the point where even the most implausible thing seemed possible, out of fear he reverted to blaming the apartment. And then he had no choice but to move.

But he did not want to move this time. He had moved three times in the last year, breaking one lease after another. He was out of money, that was part of it, yet more than that it was simply that this apartment was otherwise so perfect. Or it had been at first anyway, and maybe could be again. While with every other move he'd been able to convince himself that the next apartment would be better, that the problem was connected to his current apartment, he couldn't do that in this case. *No,* he thought, *better to make a stand here and resolve things once and for all.*

He installed locks and chains and settled in. Things kept disappearing. *Maybe,* he speculated, *there is another way into the apartment.* He scrutinized the walls closely, one after the other, tapped on them, found nothing. And yet, that didn't mean that something wasn't there.

He rented a monitoring system, a device with six cameras hidden within six identical teddy bears, and set these to record all the rooms of the apartment at night. Each camera snapped a picture every four seconds. During the day, on his computer, he'd watch at an accelerated rate the rectangle made of six small images. There he was, sleeping in his bed, moving jerkily in his sleep, the other rooms empty, never any sign of him sleepwalking, never any sign of anyone else in the apartment.

The cameras snapped a picture only every four seconds, he reminded himself. Wouldn't it be possible for a person, moving carefully and fluidly, to progress from blind spot to blind spot in such a way as to never be seen? He wasn't sleepwalking, you could see that from the way his body remained in the bed throughout the night, and that was reassuring. But there was still a chance, albeit a small one, that someone was coming in.

But how would they know when to move? How would they know that they were in a blind spot when a picture was being taken? Luck? No, it was almost certain that nobody was in the apartment.

And yet, almost certain was not quite certain.

Whoever is doing this, he thought a moment later, *is very, very clever.*

It weighed on him. Was someone there at night and he simply wasn't seeing them? Were they invisible? No, that was crazy, he couldn't think that way: nobody could be invisible. Could they? Maybe not invisible, but maybe they'd done something to make him block their image out. Hypnotized him or manipulated him in some other arcane way. Were they there on the recordings, walking back and forth with impunity right in front of his eyes? Had he been conditioned to see just an empty room?

He squinted at the monitors now, trying to see what was really there—a swash of motion, a portion of the room that was slightly off somehow. He felt as though he stared until his eyes bled. No matter how hard he stared, there was nothing there.

Over the course of the next few weeks, he left the apartment hardly at all. It had been, he reminded himself, the perfect place, and even now if he dragged himself away from the monitors and simply looked at the place without trying to look for evidence of the person hidden from him within it, he could convince himself of that again.

He hunkered down. Groceries he ordered in and had deposited in the hall before his door. He would wait until he heard the ding of the elevator signaling the delivery boy's departure, and then would dart out to grab them. On weekends, a newspaper would thump into his door and he would again wait with his ear pressed to the wood for the ding of the descending elevator before opening the door and yanking the paper in.

Most perilous was his trip down to the mailbox, a task he had performed daily at first, but now risked only once a week. This was the moment when he felt the apartment to be least secure. He would wait until the middle of the afternoon when most of the residents of the building were at work and then move as rapidly as he could: out the door with key in hand, turning the lock, then quickly to the elevator, down to the first floor, blocking the elevator door with his shoe so it wouldn't close, stretching out and quickly opening his mailbox, grabbing everything within, and then quickly upstairs again, unlocking the door and rushing back in. He could manage the whole process in two minutes on a good day, which still felt two minutes too long. But it was the best he could do.

Once he was back inside, panting, door locked behind him, he would begin to search for a trace of someone having taken advantage of his absence to break in to steal or move something. He could never find definitive evidence, yet always, a few minutes later, a few hours later, a day later, he would notice something missing.

It was on one of those trips to the mailbox that he encountered Menno. He was fairly certain that was the name the man had given. Collins had rushed from his apartment to the elevator and pressed the button and heard the winch kick on. As the elevator car was rising, he heard a door open somewhere behind him, and he glanced anxiously back, hoping the door was his, that—finally—he was going to see someone entering his apartment. But it was not his door, but rather the door across the hall. A man had come through it and was facing away now, locking it with his key.

For a moment, Collins almost rushed back into his own apartment, and well might have if the man hadn't been standing right across from Collins's door. Instead, he turned back and faced the elevator, staring dumbly at the crack between the dark-brown halves.

When the elevator dinged opened, he leaped in, repeatedly pressing the button for the ground floor.

The elevator doors began to close and he thought he was safe until a set of fingers slid into the crack and the doors shuddered and opened again. A man, smiling, stepped in.

"Ground floor?" he said, as if mistaking Collins for an elevator attendant. Collins pressed the button again, trying not to look at the man.

For a long moment, the elevator doors remained open, the man humming quietly, and then, just as they closed, he thrust his hand out at Collins. For a moment, Collins thought the man intended to strike him, then realized that he wanted him to take his hand, to shake it. When, reluctantly, he did, the man squeezed it unpleasantly hard.

"Menno," he said, or some word very much like it. It was hard for Collins to hear with precision with his hand in pain—as if, he thought, the nerves of his ears and those of his hand were intertwined. "You must be Collins," Menno said. "I'm your neighbor."

Collins muttered something noncommittal. He risked a glance at the man and saw a bluff and hearty fellow, reddish-blond hair, a face as smooth and innocent as a child's. He looked vaguely familiar. He was smiling in a way that showed none of his teeth, not even the tips. Collins had always thought there was something wrong with people who smiled without showing their teeth.

And then the elevator dinged open and Menno relaxed his grip. Collins dashed out, pressing himself against his mailbox as he fumbled with his keys. He heard Menno's slow footsteps passing behind him and moving toward the door of the building. A moment later the building door opened and Menno was gone.

In his apartment again, his perfect apartment, safe again, his back pressed to the inside of his door, he took a moment to consider Menno. He had looked familiar. Was he similar to the neighbor he had had before—not in the last place, but in the place before that?

He didn't know. Maybe. It could be. Menno looked familiar, he was sure of that, that was something.

Had that earlier neighbor been named Menno? No, he didn't think so, although to be honest he wasn't sure if he'd ever known that neighbor's name.

But this Menno was familiar, he was certain of that.

He thought about it for several days. He tried, in his mind's eye, to picture the three times he had seen that earlier neighbor in the days that had led up to his departure from that earlier apartment. At the time, he'd been certain that the earlier neighbor had been the one stealing things from him, and he had even confronted him about it. The man had been surprised and puzzled by his accusation, or at least had been very good at appearing puzzled and surprised—Collins still could not quite say which. Had the earlier neighbor looked the same as this Menno? Had he been the same person? No, Collins didn't think so, not exactly the same, but yes, he had looked similar—not the same but similar. If he'd had the foresight to take a picture of the earlier neighbor, he would know.

Menno, he thought, *what kind of a name is that?*

Which meant, perhaps, that the two neighbors were related, that one was the cousin or even brother of the other. Or, even better, that it was in fact the same person after all, but he had changed his appearance, had deliberately disguised himself.

And now, at night, as he lay waiting to fall asleep, he was seeing Menno all the time in his mind's eye, very vividly, as if a fully realized person. How was that possible? He had glimpsed the man only for a moment, a passing glance. He had not seen all of him or seen fully how he moved or how he inhabited the world, but in his mind's eye this Menno was full and complete. How had Menno gotten into his mind's eye? Didn't he have to come through his real eye to arrive there?

And in addition Collins was only seeing him in his mind's eye when he was lying down on his bed, from a prone perspective, which had nothing to do with the way he had seen Menno in the elevator. No, that prone way of seeing, that perspective, he eventually convinced himself, must mean he had seen him there, through his half-open eyes, while asleep, without knowing it.

How Menno had gotten into the apartment to stand over him, he couldn't say. How he had avoided the cameras or how he had made Collins unable to see him on the recorded images, he couldn't say either. But things were being stolen, or being moved at least, there was no disputing that. If it wasn't Menno stealing them or moving them, who could it possibly be?

Always in the past when he reached this point, he abandoned the apartment. He would wait until the dead of night and pack only a small bag and then creep away as cautiously as possible. A few days later, in a new apartment, in a new city where nobody knew him, he would start again. He had never looked back. For a while in the new apartment everything would be fine, and then things would begin to disappear again. Because, he supposed, Menno or a Menno-like person or a team of Menno-like people had once again found him.

But he could not flee this time. It was the perfect apartment, the perfect place. No, what he needed to do was pretend to leave, and to do so in broad daylight, alerting Menno, giving him a chance to follow him. He needed to lure him away from the apartment and to do it in such a way as to give Menno a chance to report the fact of his leaving to his superiors, assuming he had superiors, so that everyone involved would assume he had left.

In the apartment, looking for a missing set of playing cards he believed he remembered having owned, Collins thought it through. He would stay at the door looking out the judas until Menno opened his door. And then he, Collins, would leave the apartment as well. He would force himself to say hello to Menno. He would show Menno his bag and tell him he was leaving. Menno would no doubt feign unconcern. For good, Collins would insist, leaving for good. Once they got off the elevator, he would saunter out of the building, slowly enough that Menno would have no trouble following at a distance. And then . . . well, that was as far as he'd thought.

He kept thinking, kept looking. He looked under the sink. No cards there. He looked in the bowl of the toilet, no cards there. He looked under the bed, then between the box spring and the mattress; no cards. He moved all the cans out of the pantry, but they weren't there either.

What was there, though, at the very back of the pantry, was a gun. He almost didn't see it. It was wrapped in a cloth. It was small and snub nosed and well oiled. It was loaded. It was not his gun—he had owned a gun before, he had had a gun, though it had disappeared, been stolen or lost, at least one apartment back. And that gun, despite also being a .38, hadn't been like this gun. No, that gun had been different. It was hard to say how exactly, but it had been.

For a long time, he stared at it. *Menno must have left it here,* he told himself. Maybe Menno was planning something, was planning to use it against him. The safest thing, he told himself, was to take the gun and use it against Menno before Menno had occasion to use it against him.

He kept looking for the cards, though he knew he would never find them. Perhaps Menno was in his own apartment right now, playing solitaire with his deck, turning over every third card, surrounded by all the other things he had stolen. Once Menno was taken care of, he told himself, he needed to remember to collect his key from his pocket. Then, when he came back to the building, he could enter Menno's apartment and get his things back.

By this time his mind had figured out what to do.

Gun in his hip pocket, he would lead Menno carefully in his wake. He would leave the city and move through the suburbs and Menno would still be following him. He would walk through the suburbs and move up into the foothills and then up into the mountains.

Menno, he was sure, would still be behind him. And then, when they had reached a sufficiently isolated place, an ideal place, a *perfect* place, he would draw the pistol and shoot Menno with his own gun. And then, finally, he could retrace his steps to the perfect apartment and live there in peace.

At last it was he, rather than Menno, who was one step ahead.

He pressed his body to the door and his eye to the judas, and waited for his neighbor to appear.

—for Ian

Line of Sight

1.

The shoot had gone well—almost too well, in fact. So much so that Todd, by the end, was waiting for something to go wrong: for production to come crashing to a halt, for the union to try to shut them down with some bullshit excuse, for the lead to have his face torn halfway off in a freak accident. The longer things continued to go well, the more strongly he could feel something roiling below the surface, preparing to go badly. And the longer it didn't, the worse he felt.

He was tempted to hurt himself, just to relieve the pressure. Cut off his thumb, maybe. But he knew this wouldn't go over well with the studio. By the time they wrapped, he was jumping at every little thing: he couldn't have lasted another day. But then, suddenly, it was over, the production a wrap, and instead of being relieved he was flustered, unbelieving, still waiting for something to go wrong.

And yet, even in the early stages of postproduction, it never did. No issues with sound, no problems with editing, no problems when the footage was processed: nothing wrong. The film came out, so

174

everybody claimed, better than expected. Even though the studio had been a little standoffish with the rushes, they now claimed to love where Todd had gotten to. Unaccountably, nobody had any final notes.

"Really?" said Todd, bracing himself.

"Really," said the studio exec. "It's great as is."

"And?" said Todd.

"No ands," he said. "No buts."

Todd folded his arms. "So, what do you think needs to be changed?" he asked.

"I don't think you understand," the studio exec said. "We don't want anything changed." And then a moment later, his brow creased. "What's wrong with you? You should be celebrating."

But Todd couldn't celebrate. He was still waiting for something to go wrong.

Nothing wrong, nothing wrong, he told himself, but he still felt like he could feel the exec's eyes on his back all the way to the door, watching him go. He imagined how he would shoot that scene: a quick shot first of the exec's face, then Todd's back as he walked toward the door, then the exec's face again, expression slightly changed. He should be grateful, he knew he should—there was nothing wrong and everything right, the film was a success. But didn't that simply mean that something was likely to go hideously wrong for him on a personal level? He wasn't married, was not even *with* anybody, didn't even own a pet: what could go wrong that hadn't already? o.k., so maybe his next film would be an utter disaster? How could he enjoy this success before he knew how much it would cost him down the line?

He went home. He looked at the wall of his apartment for an hour, maybe more. It grew dark outside, then darker still. Finally, hands shaking, he drove back to the studio.

It was later than he thought. Still, he had no problem talking his way through the gate, or getting himself into the building. He got the night watchman to let him into the editing bay, then queued up the film and began to watch, pretending that he was seeing a movie directed by someone else.

It was good, he grudgingly had to admit. If he considered it objectively, he had to agree with the studio. The camerawork was excellent, startling even, the film saturated with shadow in a way that made the slow mental unraveling of the lead seem as if it were being projected all the way across the screen and even spilling off the sides a little. The effect was panicked and anxious, and he began to think that his own anxieties about the imminent collapse of the project had filtered down to everybody participating in the shoot, albeit in a way that paradoxically served the film. The lead, when he began to unravel, seemed not only like himself unraveling, but almost like a different person. It had become the kind of film that brought you close to a character and then, once that character was going mad, brought you closer still.

He stared at the empty screen, the film continuing to roll inside his head. He should be happy, he told himself. Everybody was right. He should be completely happy, and yet there was something nagging at him. What was it? The acting was excellent, the blocking and staging and camerawork just as good. Lighting was superb, sound editing was precise. What did he have to complain about?

He sighed, stretched. He should accept that the film was a success, he told himself, go home, go to bed. Instead, he queued the film up and watched it again.

The third time through, he began to sense it, began to realize what the problem was. In the interior scenes, the eyelines were a little off. Not all the interior scenes, only the ones set in the lead's childhood home, before and after he dismembered his parents. Not off by much, only slightly, not enough for anyone to notice consciously, at least not on first viewing. But who knew what it was doing subconsciously? People noticed things, it didn't matter if it was conscious or not. It needed to be fixed.

And yet, he remembered the cameraman lining all that up carefully—he'd fired the script supervisor at the cameraman's request, because the cameraman had insisted he wasn't meticulous enough about just that: eyelines. He had a vivid memory of the cameraman blocking it, then re-blocking it, making micro-movements of the camera to get it right every time they shot a scene.

He pulled up the digital files of the rough footage in the editing bay. Was he right? Even staring at a frame of the lead looking next to a frame of what, ostensibly, he was seeing, he could hardly tell. Was he imagining it? At first he thought so, but the longer he stared at it the more he thought, no, the eyelines were off.

Maybe the cameraman had a slight vision problem so that what looked right to him didn't look right to anybody else. Or maybe Todd was the one who had the vision problem and there wasn't anything there.

He toyed and tinkered with a frame a little, seeing, if he cropped and adjusted it, whether the problem could be corrected. But no matter how much he torqued it, it didn't seem to help.

It wasn't until after he had already dialed that he realized how late it was—midnight or one in the morning now. He hung up. He could wait until morning.

But, a few seconds later, his phone began to ring.

"Misdial?" the cameraman asked when he answered.

"Ah," Todd said. "You're awake. No, I meant to call. Sorry to call so late."

The cameraman didn't bother to answer, simply waited.

"It's just," said Todd. "I'm . . . the eyelines," he finally managed. "They're wrong."

For a long time, the cameraman was quiet, and Todd thought maybe he'd offended him.

"Only in the house," Todd added, as if that made it better somehow. "Everywhere else they're fine."

"Where are you?" the cameraman finally said. His voice sounded strangled.

Todd told him. "Are you o.k.?" he asked.

The man gave a laugh, part of it cut off by static from the connection. "I am now," he said. "Now that somebody else has finally noticed."

2.

"It was awful," Conrad claimed, as he and the director sat over coffee in a deserted diner at two or perhaps three in the morning. "I would set the eyelines, then look and think, yes, that's it exactly, but the whole time another part of me would be thinking, *no, not quite*. And so I would frame it again, would check everything again. Each time I would think when I looked through the viewfinder, *yes, perfect*, and then, a moment later, *but . . .*"

It had been like that through the whole shoot. Most days he thought it had something to do with the feel of the shoot as a whole, the tension present on the set for some reason. *You felt it too*, said Conrad to the director. *I could tell.* But at night, back at home, lying in bed, Conrad kept thinking back through the shots, wondering why the eyelines still didn't feel right.

"I've never felt that way," said Conrad. "I've been shooting movies for two decades and I have never felt that way."

As the shoot went on, it became not better but worse. Not outside, not in the other locations, just at the house. Conrad began to think of the house as a living thing, expanding and contracting, breathing, shifting ever so slightly. As he told this to the director he believed from the look on the man's face that he felt it too. Being in the house was like being in the belly of something. It was like they'd been swallowed, and that the house, seemingly inert, was not inert at all. It was always shifting ever so slightly, so that even in the time it took to go from a shot of a face looking at something to setting up a shot to reveal where that face was looking, everything was already slightly wrong, slightly off.

"It sounds crazy," said the director.

"Yes," Conrad agreed. "It sounds crazy. But you felt it, too."

And it was even worse than that, Conrad claimed. For when he had stared, really stared, it seemed like something was beginning to open up, like if he stood just right he could see a seam where reality had been imperfectly fused. He had stood there on the balls of his feet, swaying slightly, not caring what the crew around him might think. And then, for an instant, he even managed to see it just right, not so much a threadlike seam as a narrow opening, as well as someone—or some*thing* rather—gazing out.

"Why didn't you tell me?" asked the director.

Conrad shrugged. "You've said it yourself," he said. "It sounded crazy. And you didn't say anything either. The film editor didn't notice it at all. But then, he wasn't on the set, was he?"

The director hesitated, then nodded. Both men sat in silence and sipped their coffee. Finally the director said, "What was it?"

"Excuse me?" asked Conrad.

"Gazing out," said the director. "What was it?"

Conrad shook his head. "I don't know for certain what it was," he said. "All I know is what it looked like."

"And what did it look like?" the director asked, though the look on his face said that he didn't want to know.

You had to understand, Conrad claimed, that what it looked like was probably not what it was. That if he had to guess, it was the sort of thing that took on aspects of other things that came close to it, a kind of mimic of anything it could manage to approach. In a house like that, in a place where the seam of the fabric of reality was wrongly annealed, it would take on the appearance of whatever it had the chance to observe, to study through the gap in the seam. "At first I thought I was wrong," said Conrad, "that I was seeing some sort of odd reflection or refraction, that I couldn't be seeing two things that looked the same. But when they each moved they moved in a way that couldn't be seen as either the same or as mirroring one another. No, even though they looked identical, they were anything but the same."

The director struck the tabletop hard with his open palm. "Goddamn it," he said, "what did it look like?"

Conrad looked surprised. How was it the director hadn't guessed? "Why, the lead, of course."

3.

The whole production Steven Calder (née Amos Smith) had had the feeling that something was wrong. Not with him, not with his acting, no, that was good. As good as it had ever been in fact, for reasons that he wasn't sure he could understand. Not with the director either, though the man was an odd one, jumpy as fuck. Cameraman was o.k., too, if a bit anal, and so were the rest of the crew. No, nothing visibly wrong anywhere, nothing he could place the blame on. Just a feeling.

He shrugged it off and kept going, acting like everything was fine. Or, rather, acting like he was losing his mind, which was what the film was about, him losing his mind, his character losing his mind, though when the camera wasn't rolling, yes, then, acting like everything was fine, even racking his brains for dumb jokes he'd heard back in high school—or rather, things that the Amos Smith he'd used to be had heard back in high school—things he could throw out to lighten the mood, things meant to demonstrate that he was at ease and nothing was wrong.

But he certainly was not at ease. And something *was* wrong, he was sure of it. In the house meant to represent his parents' house especially. Meant to represent his *character's* parents' house, he meant. Outside, no, he didn't feel it—nor, strangely enough, did he feel it in the other indoor locations, yet in the house, yes, there he felt it. It made him feel seasick, as though the floor was shifting slightly under his feet, but that was crazy, houses didn't act like that.

But that was how this house acted. At least for him. Was he the only one who could feel something was wrong?

Steven was most sure something was wrong at those moments when he stood at his mark in the house meant to represent his parents' house—meant to represent his *character's* parents' house—and waited for the scene to be shot. The lighting was adjusted, the camera positioned, and the whole time he just stood there. Soon, he would think, maybe even as early as his next film, someone else would stand on his mark for him, a body double, though for now it was him. This was his big break, he was the lead, but until the break had broken it would be him standing in for himself.

At those moments, standing on his mark, sometimes he felt he could see, there beside him, a flickering, a strangeness in the air. But if he turned his head to look straight at it, he couldn't see it anymore. And then the cameraman would scold him mildly, coax him back to looking in the direction he had originally been meant to look, and the flicker would begin again. What was it? The rapid oscillation of the ceiling lights, maybe? Something wrong with his brain? He couldn't say. He didn't think it was something with his brain, but if it wasn't, why didn't anyone else seem to see it?

It happened about three-quarters of the way through shooting, right in the middle of the murder scene. There he was, the dismembered bodies of what were meant to be his parents at his feet. He was still breathing hard, hyperventilating slightly, his vision fading a little, spattered in what would pass on film for blood, and he saw what he'd come to think of as a flicker. Only this time it was more than a flicker, more like a rip in the air, like an animal had torn the air open with its teeth. The cameraman was seeing something too. There was a strange expression on his face, and he was looking at the air right beside Steven's head with a sort of mute wonder. *Don't move*, something inside him said, and he could feel the hair rising on the back of his neck. He held still, very still indeed.

There was a smell like ozone, bitter and deep in his throat, the sound of something unfurling, and then he could feel breath hot on his neck. In front of him, the cameraman moved abnormally slowly, as if walking underwater. And then, abruptly, he was jerked, hard and fast, off his feet, the air knocked out of him.

By the time he had pulled himself up, a few seconds later, the room was empty. The camera was gone, the entire crew as well, the room deserted. How was that possible?

"Hello?" Steven called, but there was no answer.

He got up and walked around the room. No sign, as far as he could see, of where they had gone. No sign, if he was to be honest with himself, which he was not sure he wanted to be, that the production team had ever been here: camera gone, lighting gone, none of the cables or other apparatuses of a shoot. *What the hell?* he thought.

He walked around the room another time, and then again, growing more and more anxious. He tried the other rooms and found them just as deserted, just as silent. He called out and listened for a response, but there was no response. Finally, he went through the front door and left the house.

Or at least he would have, if there'd been anything to go out into. There was nothing outside of the house, the door opening onto nothing at all.

How long had he been there? How many days? A long time, it felt like, though in another sense it felt like almost no time at all. He had tried all the doors and windows. It was always the same: there was nothing outside the house. He wasn't hungry, which confused him. He wasn't sure how he could still be alive. Assuming he actually was.

He sat with his back to the wall, watching, waiting. Looking down at the backs of his hands he could see through them the ebb and flow of his blood. How strange. Had he been able to see that before? It was as if his skin was becoming transparent. He got up and paced, back and forth, back and forth, then sat down again. He slept for a while, woke, slept again, woke, went back to sleep.

He was just stretching, getting up again, when he caught a glimpse of it—that same flickering he had seen before. Immediately he was on his feet and looking for it, searching for it in the air. He swept his fingers back and forth but found nothing: there was nothing there. And yet, when he turned away, there it was, in the corner of his vision, flickering, again.

He moved toward it slowly, not looking directly at it so as not to startle it. He followed it as best he could, backing toward it, head down.

And then, from one moment to the next, his vision shifted, the flicker becoming a line of light, a line that opened until it became a slit and he could see something through it.

He was looking at the house, at another version of the house. This one had the production crew in it. The camera was rolling, and there he was as well, axe trailing from one hand, breathing heavily, his shirt spattered with blood. He watched the scene come to an end, watched as he, his character, killed both his parents, watched until the director said cut.

Only then did the figure that was meant to be him relax and glance his way, looking right at him, straight through the narrow gap. For a moment, they both regarded one another and then the other him smiled in a way that bared his teeth, and Steven realized that what he was seeing not only wasn't him after all, it wasn't even human.

Through the slit he'd watched the film wrap, watched them pack all the equipment up, watched whatever it was that had taken his place genially shake hands with everybody and then head out the door, out to live his life. The rest of the crew went too. When the last crewmember had turned off the light, the opening faded.

There followed a long period in which nothing happened, where it was only he himself alone. His body grew longer, leaner. He didn't sleep anymore, though he sometimes lay down and pretended to sleep. He was hungry all the time but not for food exactly—for what he didn't precisely know. The flicker maybe, or what it led to. He wandered the house, looking again for that flicker, but it just wasn't there. Maybe it was still there, though if it was, he couldn't find it.

Or couldn't anyway, until something changed. There it was, the flickering, and there he was, slowly moving toward it while trying to give the impression of moving away, until, finally, he had found the slit again. There it was, he could see it, the twin of the house he was now trapped in, dimly lit by the beams of two flashlights flickering their way through the dark space.

"It's got to be around here somewhere," said a voice, one he was pretty sure he recognized.

"Are you sure it's a good idea?" asked the other voice, also familiar.

He wasn't the one being asked, he knew, but he was sure it was a good idea. Maybe not for these two men, but definitely for him. Whoever *he* was, now. He could already feel his body changing, becoming more and more like whichever of the two men he looked at the most.

"Even if we do find it, how are we going to get through it?" asked the second voice.

Steven had an answer for this question too. He waited patiently for them to find the slit. When they did, well, they'd have no problem getting through it, because he would help them. Would help one of them anyway. The problem for that one would not be getting in, as he knew from experience, but getting out again.

Trigger Warnings

Caution: self-harming behavior. Caution: depictions of war. Caution: depictions of self-harming behavior in a war-torn nation, probably Serbia (unless you are Serbian). Caution: severed head. Caution: self-severing of own head, depicted in slow motion. Caution: unrealistic situation of violence, such as is often depicted in manga. Caution: theatrical violence inflicted upon midgets. Caution: ghosts. Caution: flaming ghosts (as in ghosts on fire, not flamboyantly gay ghosts). Caution: gay ghosts. Caution: spiders. If you have a severe spider phobia (talking to you, Debbie—you need help!) you should stay the fuck away from this story. Caution: profanity. Caution: Mormons. Caution: realistic depictions of Mormons, as missionaries, coming to a door much like your own door. If you are afraid of Mormons, please ask for an alternate reading assignment! Caution: depictions of shell-shocked Mormon missionaries going door to door in a war-torn nation as bombs fall around them. Nobody opens the door for them. One of them—caution!—sees what he thinks is a ball on the ground, but it turns out to be a human head. Before his mind registers that this is actually a head and not a ball, he has kicked it. Later, he will be haunted by the head of a ghost, potentially gay, that once resided in the head that he kicked, and this ghost-head will summon spiders, thousands and thousands of spiders (stay away, Debbie!). Caution: amputees. Caution: if you are afraid of amputees, please avoid this story. Caution: if you are an amputee, please trust that I did not intend to insult you or your ilk (probably an unfortunate choice of words, since *ilk* sounds like a part of a word rather than a whole word), and please do not feel obligated to read this story. But, if you, an amputee, do read the story, please know I would gladly welcome any suggestions from you as per what the life of an amputee is really like. Like, how do you tie your shoes, for instance (or shoe, if you only have one leg)? Caution: psychiatrists. There are hundreds of psychiatrists in this story, and each of them has a catchphrase they repeat over and over. Reading this story <u>will make you hate psychiatrists, *even if you are a psychiatrist*</u>. Caution: flaming ghosts of Mormon amputee psychiatrists. Unless they are in fact psychotherapists. I forget which is the one with the medical degree. Maybe neither (caution: lack of verified medical knowledge). Their amputation is their head, each has had their head amputated, if that's a word you can use to describe a head being separated from the body, and each carries their "amputated" head under their arm, though sometimes they set down their head and later pick up the wrong head. Caution: references to video games. Caution: excessive violence not unlike that found in the video game you were playing a few minutes before picking up this assigned story. Do yourself a favor: go back to the video game and remain untraumatized. Caution: men in trees. Caution: excessive use of exclamation marks! Caution!!!! Caution: colostomy bags vs. frat boys (hint: nobody wins). Caution: limber, self-fellating Smurfs. Caution: excessive and profane use of the color blue: IF YOU READ MY SMURF PORNOGRAPHY, BLUE WILL NEVER BE THE SAME FOR YOU AGAIN: ONLY READ THIS IF YOU ARE BLUE-CURIOUS AND PRE-PARED TO JOIN US! Caution: cute kittens. Caution: references to social media. Caution: if you are over forty-five, you will not under-stand that these references are to actual social media platforms and will judge this story, which is a *realistic* story, to be some sort of science fiction, thus revealing yourself to be *too old*. Caution: I am not an SF writer, and if I get any more of your namby-pamby workshop comments saying that I write "sci-fi" I will take you outside and cut your shit up. Caution: profanity. Caution: biologically improbable sexual situations. If you try to reenact these situations at home, you will at best sprain something and at worst wind up in the emergency room with an earnest ER resident explaining the surprising strength (sometimes against its own interest) of the muscle known as the sphincter while secretly taking pictures that he will later post on a social media platform that, mercifully, you have never heard of. Caution: unrealistic characters. Caution: white men from the Midwest. Unless you are Jonathan Franzen (and if so, my condolences), you will find the men in these stories reprehensible. Caution: God, but God's a woman. Or rather—*caution!!!*—just became a woman: God in this story is trans, but hell, if you've watched pay cable in the last year you'll probably be O.K. Caution: Colin Hanks depicted trying to act. Caution: midgets. Did I already do that one? No, it was Mormons. Same difference, really. Caution: cultural insensitivity. Caution: republicans. Caution: an army of republican Mexican-wrestling midgets led by Colin Hanks face off against flaming amputee Mormon ghost psychiatrists in my story "Hymn-Off," with each army trying to sing hymns better than the other, as judged by trans-God. For those who feel they would be wounded by this story, I have included a version that has no Mormons and no republicans and instead takes place in a public high school in California with competing midget glee clubs. Trans-God is still the judge. Caution: eighties music. Caution: feathered hair. Caution: fiction.

Kindred Spirit

1.

At first there is me and there is my sister, and then there is only me. Or rather, to put it more precisely, first there is me and I am observing my sister, for my sister is unstable. It is hard, sometimes, to believe we are siblings, and sometimes I, the stable one, do not believe so. *Your task,* my father says—if he really is my father—*is to watch her, to observe her.* If he is my father then he is probably not my sister's father—which I suppose would make my sister something other than my sister. Perhaps she is my half sister, and we share the same mother. But we have never known a mother. Perhaps, as my sister used to suggest before her death, we were grown in a vat, not a womb.

Perhaps I, the stable sister, am not quite as stable as I have been led to believe.

To return to the matter at hand, my sister sits in a chair that is too large. Or, more precisely, it is a normal-sized chair, even though my sister is too small for a normal-sized chair. I, too, am too small for the normal-sized chair I am sitting in, which is positioned right beside my sister's. Neither my sister nor myself are normal sized. In this, at least, we are alike.

We both stare at the blank wall. It is a whitewashed wall with a crack wandering across it. Sometimes I feel this crack hides a face. There are two larger holes where perhaps nails were once affixed, presumably to hang a picture. But there has never been a picture hanging on this wall in my lifetime.

My sister and I awkwardly grip the arms of our normal-sized chairs and stare in mutual silence at the wall.

From time to time, I cast a sidelong glance at my sister, to assure myself that she is still present in the chair beside me. It is my task to watch her. So says Father. As far as I can tell, she does not glance at me. Perhaps she does not care if I am still there. Perhaps, unlike me, she does not have a task.

I hear the buzzing of a fly. The creature passes before my eyes, a disruption in the air, and then circles, humming, above my head. It is behind my chair, then beside it, then comes to settle on the chair's arm.

Carefully, I lift one hand, slowly, slowly. Then I bring it down swiftly, killing the fly, cracking the chair's arm in the process. I am, as my father has noted, exceptionally strong and exceptionally swift—another sign, so my sister might suggest, that at least one of us—me—was grown in a vat.

I flick the dead fly onto the floor. Half smiling, I turn to my sister, eager for her to acknowledge what I have done.

But my sister is no longer beside me. While I have been engaged with the fly, she has left her chair and traveled to the far side of the room, clambering up into the open window. She is framed in it. As I watch, she throws herself out. By the time I have reached the window myself, she lies in the courtyard below, blood spreading in a puddle around her head.

I do what any faithful sister would do: I leap out after her.

...

When I come to myself again, I am lying beside my sister. The cobblestones where my body struck are cracked and buckled. I am unharmed, so far as I can determine. How can I be unharmed?

My sister's eyes are open. For a moment I think she is still alive. But she is not alive. She is dead. I have failed in my task.

I do not know how long I lie there. Perhaps an hour, perhaps two. Long enough for the blood to stop pooling and to become tacky: it sticks to the side of my head and dries there. Long enough for my father to come looking for us and find us no longer in the room. Long enough for him to peer out the window and see us both lying in the courtyard, one of us dead, the other pretending to be dead, and to cry out.

"You had one task," my father tells me. My sister's body has been carried away, the blood scrubbed from the stones. I have been washed and brought back here, to this room. As I sit in the normal-sized chair, he walks back and forth, his hands clasped behind his back. "You failed in your task," he says.

"I failed," I acknowledge. I bow my head.

"I no longer have a daughter," he says.

"You no longer have *two* daughters," I correct. "You still have me."

He hesitates a moment, finally nods. His hesitation is not lost on me, nor is the fact that after I speak he seems confused then afraid, though I am not sure what I am to learn from this.

He walks back and forth. "How am I to know that you did not push her?"

"Why would I hurt my sister?" I say. "She jumped and then I jumped after her."

"Why would you jump after her?"

"I was hoping to catch her," I lie. "Absorb her fall." But I was too far behind her to do that or even believe that it might be possible. The truth is I was hoping to be like her, to be dead with her. But I failed in that as well.

My father stares at me. "I wonder . . . ," he says absently. "What distracted you? What made you stop watching her?"

"A fly," I say.

"A fly?" he says, surprised. "But there are no flies in this place. How do you even know about flies?"

I look on the floor for the dead fly, but there is nothing there. Could I have imagined it?

"I saw a fly, Father," I insist.

"Don't call me that," he says sharply. "Impossible," he adds. Then he sighs. "What shall I do with you? Shall I store you?"

"Store me?" I ask, confused.

"Never mind," he says. He waves his fingers. "Carry on," he says, and leaves the room.

But how am I to carry on? I had one task, as my father has always pointed out to me. Now that my sister is dead, I have no task at all. What am I to do with myself?

I spend a certain amount of time in the room, sitting in my normal-sized chair. If I look only at the wall, letting my eyes drift along the crack, there are moments, brief moments, when I can imagine the face of my sister caught in the crack and then I can extract it and float it away from the wall to reside here beside me. I can feel her. It is as if we are both still alive and together in the room.

But then I turn my head and she is not there. I am alone.

But does it have to be me? Why must I think of myself as me and not as her, as my sister? In so many ways we were so alike, weren't we? Could I not be her? Would it not be possible for me to shift my thinking slightly and become the unstable one, the one who needs to be watched?

After all, I already know I am not as stable as I have been led to believe. How hard could it possibly be to no longer be me?

2.

I leave the room. When I come back, I sit not in the normal-sized chair with the broken arm but in the other chair, the one closer to the window. *This is my chair,* I insist to myself. *That other chair belongs to my sister.*

I take my place and wait for my sister to enter. She will sit beside me and, as she always does, observe me. Why does she observe me? Because my father has told her to do so. But why would she listen to my father? And what manner of creature is she? Why is it that, though I am told repeatedly she is my sister, I have a hard time believing it?

When my sister does not appear, I close my eyes. I empty my mind of all thoughts. And then, slowly, I allow there to enter, from somewhere deep within my skull, the sound of footsteps. They move from the doorway past me, a child's step but heavier than my own. And then I hear her take her place in the chair next to me.

I open my eyes. I do not look at her. I look instead at the wall across from me. It is enough to know my sister is there, looking at me, keeping me safe.

Or is it? What is she keeping me safe from? She looks like me and she does not look like me. Is she really my sister? Why does my father insist we call one another sisters? She is not encased in flesh but in some other substance that resembles flesh.

Once, a man broke into our room brandishing a weapon. He aimed it at me and fired, but my sister, impatient and quick, was already in front of me, shielding me with her own body, moving with a speed I did not believe her capable of. When the weapon discharged, it tore a hole in her flesh but revealed something unexpected beneath: another, harder rind that the discharge blackened but could not pierce. I remember that the man appeared first surprised and then very afraid. *What in God's name are you?* I believe he managed to say. A moment later, moving even faster, my sister had done a sequence of things to the man that, by its end, left him little more than a sodden sack of meat. Like me, to his detriment, he did not have a harder rind beneath his skin.

I remember my father questioning my sister. Why, he wanted to know, had she done that to the man? Why hadn't she kept him alive so that he could be questioned and we could determine which of my father's enemies had been responsible? Did she think it was easy to govern in a place like this, so alien, so far away from the comforts of home? *Perhaps you need to be recalibrated,* my father said, half to himself.

If we are so different inside, beneath our skin, how can we be sisters? Surely we cannot be true sisters. But why would my father want us to address one another in this way?

Perhaps for her benefit; perhaps for mine.

No, certainly for hers.

I finger the skin on my belly. There is a slight irregularity to the skin there, from where the man shot me. I sink my fingers in and feel my harder rind beneath.

For of course, I am not my sister after all. I am just me. It does not matter what chair I sit in: a self cannot be shrugged on and off so easily as that.

Or, at least, if it can, it can be only for a moment.

I return to my chair, the one with the broken arm, broken by me. I close my eyes and try again to imagine my sister alive and beside me.

It is harder imagining her alive than it was imagining I was her. But in the end, if I keep my eyes closed I can do it. I can hear her opening the door. I can hear the sound of her steps, so much lighter than my own, as they cross the floor. I can hear the whisper of her soft limbs as they brush against the wood as she climbs up into her chair.

I revel in this moment of my sister being alive again.

Then I hear the buzz of a fly.

. . .

I hear it in front of me, behind me, above me. I keep my eyes tightly closed. I will the sound to go away.

But the sound does not go away. It maintains itself, a buzz and then a whine. And then I hear the thunk of a heavy hand slamming down, killing it, breaking the arm of the chair.

I open my eyes and see my sister, alive again, crouched in the window, ready to throw herself out. And then with a cry she does.

And here am I tumbling out into the air after her.

3.

When I come conscious, I am not in the courtyard. I am on a metal table, a bank of lights above me, burning brilliantly. Two men in white coats and surgical masks loom beside me. They are turned away from me and hunched over a set of instruments and parts, making choices. One of them, despite the way he is swaddled, I recognize as my father.

A large round mirror is on a telescoping arm next to me. Before they notice I am awake, I adjust it so that I can see myself in it.

In the reflection, parts of my face have been loosened, the skin peeled back to reveal the rind beneath. There is a square opening in my forehead and deep within I see a dim, throbbing glow.

My father turns around. With his tools he begins to reassemble my face. I remain still, as if, like my sister, I am dead.

"I don't understand," says my father to the man next to him. "Misprogramming? Some sort of bug? Why is it seeing things that aren't there?"

The other man shrugs. "There is so much we don't know," he says. "Once activated, they begin to learn for themselves, in their own way. Maybe something is wrong, or maybe this is simply what happens."

"Do you think it killed her?" my father asks.

The other man hesitates. "I . . . don't think so," he says. "The bond strikes me as too close, too personal for that."

"What do I do with it?" asks my father as he continues to layer my face back into place. "Reset it? Then I lose anything it knows about my daughter's death."

"I don't know," says the man.

"Is it dangerous?"

"Of course it's dangerous," the man says. "But not dangerous to you."

It is at this moment that I reach out and take hold of my father's wrist. I do it very quickly but very carefully, and yet he still winces.

"Father," I say.

"Yes," he says. He is trying to keep his voice calm. The other man has stepped back and away. He presses his back against the wall.

"What is that man's name?" I ask.

"Jensen," my father manages.

"Tell Jensen to do nothing rash," I say. "Perhaps he should sit down on the floor and put his hands on his head and just wait."

Father looks at the other man, and nods. Slowly the man does as I have asked.

"I don't intend to hurt anyone," I say.

"That's good," my father says. "I am very glad to hear that."

"But we need to have a frank conversation. Will you be frank with me?"

He hesitates, and then nods.

"You are not my father," I say.

"No," he says. "Not per se."

"Do I have a father?"

"No," he says. "In one sense, the closest thing you have to a father is me, but you do not have a father."

I nod. "Good," I say. "Yes, I knew that," I say. "Somehow I knew that. Shall we talk about my sister?"

"You weren't . . . exactly her sister," he says.

"No," I say.

"More like a . . . kindred spirit."

"A kindred spirit."

"Like sisters without ever really being sisters."

"Was she afraid of me?"

"I don't know," says my father. "You were there to protect her, so she should not have been. But perhaps she still was. Do you think that is why she leaped from the window?"

I do not answer. I let go of his wrist. "I need a moment to think," I say. "Can you give me a moment?"

My father nods. He helps the other man to his feet and together, furtively, the pair of them leave the room.

I look at my face in the mirror. Parts of it are closed and look like my sister's face. Other parts are open, revealing the rind and even something throbbing beneath the rind. *Kindred spirit,* I think. What does that mean precisely? Someone who is like you, who acts like you, thinks like you, resembles you in the most important ways. But what happens to the kindred spirit when the person they resemble is gone? Who are they kindred to then?

I leave my face as it is, partly open, partly closed. Like this, variegated, it better represents me, who I am, what I am feeling.

And what am I to do now? I can wait here for my father who is not my father to come back, bringing with him a contingent of armed men who will try—and no doubt succeed—to disable me. Or I can do as my sister did. I can still show that I am her kindred spirit, and leap out the window.

I shall keep in pursuit of my dead sister, my kindred spirit. I will not rest until, like her, I too am dead.

Lather of Flies

"Shall I explain how this usually works?" asked Lahr. He sat in a brocaded wingback chair, a half smile on his face, head resting lazily against the soiled antimacassar as if there were no bones in his neck. Motes of dust whirled through the dim light around his hairless head. Tilton was perched precariously on a rickety low bench across from him.

"Usually you or someone not unlike you asks me a series of questions about my career before bringing yourself to mention *the film*. I show surprise. I tell you there is no such film to be found, we argue back and forth. Eventually I suggest, offhandedly, that you might, oh, if it really interests you that much, undertake an examination of a certain private archive. Not that there's likely anything there, I warn you, but just in case—no stone left unturned and all that. You, elated, rush away, and manage through your ingenuity to force your way into said archive, only to discover nothing." Lahr shrugged. "Perhaps, undaunted, you return here, to me. Perhaps you are deluded enough to believe it has all been some sort of test, a way for me to ascertain how *serious* you really are about *the film*. Whether you are serious enough to be included among the half dozen or so people who have experienced—or, I should say, allegedly experienced—the film. Perhaps, then, I suggest another archive, another possibility, and you again rush off in pursuit."

With some effort, Lahr lifted his head.

"Shall we play it that way? Or will you accept now my plain assertion that there is no film to be found?"

"You never shot it," said Tilton.

"I didn't say that," said Lahr, tone suddenly sharp. "I said there is no film to be found. Quite a different thing."

"Different how?" asked Tilton. And when Lahr didn't bother to answer, tried, "So there was only rough footage?"

Lahr gave the slightest, feeblest shrug. "No film to be found," he repeated.

"But it *was* shot," said Tilton. "You did shoot it."

"In a manner of speaking," said Lahr.

"You destroyed it?"

"Why ever would I do that? I'm not an idiot."

Tilton, feeling more and more uncomfortably perched, was confused. "I don't understand."

Lahr smiled. "Ah," he said, "you see? That's how it begins."

For Tilton, though, it had begun some time before. Despite being a PhD candidate in film studies, he had first heard mention of the film in a bar. From a stranger, very drunk, seated beside him, who kept slipping off his stool and then clambering back up again. The stranger kept introducing himself. It was almost like a slapstick routine. Tilton humored him for a time, until eventually he tired of it and stopped speaking to the man, turning slightly away.

The drunk gave a barking laugh. "Cold shoulder?" he said. "To me? To *me*? Don't you know why I'm here?" And then the stranger grabbed his shoulder, squeezed it hard.

Tilton looked desperately for the bartender, who was at the far end of the bar.

"Not so cold," the man said, mostly to himself. "Not so cold. Human mostly. At least so far."

"What's that supposed to mean?" asked Tilton, without quite looking into the man's face.

"It speaks," said the man, and released his shoulder.

"All right, then," said Tilton, "why *are* you here?"

"Don't mind me," said the man. "I'm not worth listening to, mostly. Except when I am." He made Tilton wait a few moments before going on, pointing eventually at Tilton's shoulder bag. "You're a professor," he accused.

Tilton shook his head. "Grad student."

"What field?"

"Film studies."

"Ah," said the man. "You've heard of Lahr?"

"The filmmaker?" asked Tilton, and only now turned toward the stranger again.

The man eyed him shrewdly, with a calculating air. Suddenly he seemed hardly drunk at all. "What other Lahr is there?"

"How do you know about him?" asked Tilton.

"How do you?" asked the man. "You're young. Nobody watches Lahr's stuff anymore. Why do you?"

For a long time afterward, Tilton was not sure how much of what the stranger next told him was true. His name was Serno, so he said, and he claimed to have worked with Lahr. When Tilton looked it up, he found that there was indeed an actor by that name, a minor one. He had worked on two of Lahr's films: *River of Blood* and *Angel of Death*. In the first he was identified as *dead cowboy #1* and in the second as *bleeding man*—exactly as the stranger had told him in the bar once he'd realized Tilton was a "film aficionado." Tilton didn't remember Serno from either film. Later, rewatching them, he was far from certain that the man he was seeing was the same man he had met in the bar.

"Happy to have been part of them. Two good films," claimed Serno, "or good enough. Since neither is hardly Lahr's masterpiece."

"His masterpiece," said Tilton. "*Slow Orchids*, you mean."

The man gave a little laugh of derision. "Hardly," he said. *"Lather of Flies."*

Lather of Flies? He wasn't a Lahr specialist, not remotely, and yet he'd seen all of Lahr's films—or thought he had. "I don't know *Lather of . . .* ," he started, then stopped, racking his brain. "Perhaps I would know it under another name?"

"No," said the man. "There is no other name. *Lather of Flies.*"

"But—" he frowned. He got out his phone, searched for the title. "You're sure it's one of Lahr's?"

"Positive."

Tilton showed him his phone's screen. "No sign of its existence," he said.

"Oh, but it does exist," said Serno. "I should know. I'm in it."

"Was it not released?" asked Tilton. "Some sort of distribution problem, maybe?"

The man lifted his glass, drained the dregs.

"Something like that. Excuse me a moment," he said. He rose precariously to his feet and wove his way toward the bathroom.

Lather of Flies, thought Tilton; he shrugged. Probably the man was winding him up to get a free beer or two.

Which was why Tilton wasn't surprised when, after ten minutes, the man had not reappeared. He'd already finished his drinks, so why bother to come back? He'd gotten what he wanted. Tilton paid the bill and got up to leave.

But then, for reasons he didn't, until later, quite understand, he instead found himself walking toward the bathroom in search of the man.

There was a stench when he opened the bathroom door, not the usual latrine reek but something different: heated dust, irradiated air, ozone. The room's lights were off, the space vaguely illuminated by a bank of windows set in the walls directly behind and above the toilet stalls.

He turned on the light. The fluorescents flickered a little then stabilized, stayed on, humming.

"Hello?" he said. And then, "Serno?" Even though he was not altogether convinced this was the man's actual name.

No answer came.

He opened the first stall, found it empty. The second was empty too. So was the third, except for a long swath of blood behind the toilet, running up the wall to the half-open window.

He didn't know for certain, he eventually told himself, that this was Serno's blood. It could have been there for some time. Or no, not *some time* since it was red rather than brown, and looked wet. He reached out and touched it, and his fingers came away bloody.

"Something's happened in the bathroom," he told the bartender. The latter nodded. He began rooting around behind the bar, eventually coming up with a plunger.

"Nothing like that," Tilton said. "Not a clog. I think someone might be dead."

"If somebody's nodded out, call 911," said the bartender.

"It's not that. Come on," said Tilton.

The bartender sighed. He was too busy to go, he claimed, and he didn't want to see—particularly if it was someone actually dead rather than simply passed out. But in the end he came all the same.

By the time they reached the bathroom, the blood was gone. Maybe someone had quickly cleaned up, licking the wall until it sparkled (*Where the hell did that thought come from?* Tilton wondered). Or maybe the blood had never been there at all. He examined his fingers: spotlessly clean.

He went home, conducted more substantive research on Serno. The two Lahr films he had mentioned were the only things he seemed to have acted in. Serno was a pseudonym, though none of his reference books or online sources seemed to know what the man's actual name was. All they knew was that this name, Serno, was false. In addition, at least according to one source, Serno had been missing for nearly two decades. Long ago he had been presumed dead.

All of which had propelled him to Lahr, to ask about *Lather of Flies*, the film that Serno had mentioned that perhaps did and perhaps did not exist.

"Serno," Lahr mused. "Of course I remember him. He was my first and foremost dead cowboy in *River of Blood*. Not much of an actor, although he could play a dead body like nobody's business." He tented his fingers, sighed. "Ah, Serno. That's not his real name, you know."

"What *is* his real name?"

Lahr shrugged. "Does it really matter?"

"I don't know," said Tilton. "Why would he go to such lengths to hide it?"

"I thought it was *Lather of Flies* you were here about. Is it instead this fellow Serno? Are you going off script?"

Tilton shook his head. "I'm here about the movie," he said.

With great effort Lahr rose from his chair and made his way to the desk. He scribbled something on a scrap of paper. With shaking fingers he held the scrap out to Tilton.

"You might try here," he said. "Not that there's likely anything," he warned, "but just in case—no stone unturned and all that." And then he smiled in a way that, for an instant, made Tilton's skin crawl.

He left Lahr's house thinking, *There's no point visiting the archive— Lahr himself all but said so.* He should, he told himself, simply go home, continue with his studies, and forget all about it. That would be the sensible thing.

And yet something tugged at him. His mind calmly imagined returning to his normal life while his body, seemingly autonomous, boarded a bus. He could remember boarding the bus and getting off of it, but nothing about the ride itself, as if he had sunk too deeply into his thoughts to actually experience it. Indeed, he was surprised to find himself standing on the sidewalk, the bus pulling away from him in a roar of exhaust as he compared the address on the paper to that on the door in front of him and found they matched.

Where am I? he thought hopelessly. *What's happening to me?*

And then, since, after all, he was already there, he opened the door and stepped inside.

"No," the tweed-suited archivist behind the marble counter said. "Visitors simply aren't allowed in unless they inquire in writing and are granted approval from the board. That process takes weeks, sometimes months."

"I see," said Tilton. "Well, thank you for your time."

But when he turned to leave, the archivist reached out and grasped the arm of Tilton's jacket. "I'm very sorry," he said. "You'll have to leave."

"I am—I was already leaving," said Tilton, surprised. He struggled and failed to shake his arm free.

It was as if the man hadn't heard. He came around from behind his counter and steered Tilton toward the door. But instead of ushering him out, the archivist opened the door inward and hid Tilton behind it, so he was still in the room, just hidden. He smoothed his hands over Tilton's jacket again and again until he seemed assured that Tilton would remain standing where he was. And then he stepped away.

What the hell? wondered Tilton.

He moved his head a little so as to peer around the edge of the door. The archivist had his back turned to Tilton now. He was tidying his counter while standing on the customers' side. A moment later, he leaned far across the counter. When he came back up he was holding his briefcase.

When the archivist turned toward him, Tilton quickly ducked his head behind the door again. He listened to the sound of the archivist's footsteps, the sharp echoic crack of his heels against the marble floor, the sound growing harsher as the archivist moved closer.

And then the door swung away and left him exposed.

Or he would have been exposed if there had been anyone in the room to be exposed to. For the archivist was now on the far side of the door, already turning the key in the lock, leaving for the day, locking Tilton in.

He wanted me here, he told himself later as he moved through the rows of metal shelves, looking at case after case for a series that might contain the reels of *Lather of Flies. Why else would he have done what he did?* Sometimes he would take a case down if the title written on it seemed unclear or improbable, and open it to see if the title on the reel matched the case's label. Sometimes he would even examine a few feet of film until he could verify the title.

He tried not to think about what had happened with the archivist. *Ingenious method,* he imagined Lahr saying. He tried to push the voice down.

But down where? Where was there for the voice to go?

After seven or eight hours, he gave up. He was certain *Lather of Flies* was not in this archive. He could not figure a way out through the locked door, though, and so he sat in one corner and closed his eyes.

He was awakened a few hours later, morning light streaming in through the now-open door. The furious archivist was shaking him. "How did you get in here!" the man was saying. His anger and puzzlement seemed genuine. "Out!" he said. "Out! Before I have you arrested!"

Lahr's house. *Cut to Lahr's house,* thought the exhausted Tilton. He was tired and hungry, his hair disordered, his clothing rumpled, and yet here he was, back for more.

"Back for more?" asked Lahr, brightly. "No luck?" He was in the same brocaded chair as before but seemed different somehow. Held himself differently, seemed stronger than before. Perhaps he did better in the mornings, slowly losing his energy over the course of the day. Or perhaps he had been ill yesterday and today had recovered.

How old was Lahr anyway? Tilton was startled to find he couldn't remember. Quite old, no doubt. Surely at that age people had as many good days as bad.

Lahr was staring expectantly at him as if waiting for him to speak. How much time had gone by? Had he phased out at some point?

"No luck," he finally managed.

"I thought as much," said Lahr. "Ingenuity helps you not at all if there's nothing awaiting you. Tell me, how did you get past the archivist? He's a stickler for etiquette, that one."

"I . . . don't know," said Tilton. The story of what had happened now seemed so improbable to him as to be unreal.

Lahr's eyes were very bright. "That's that then," he said. "You tried. Nobody can say you didn't. Back to school, eh?"

Tilton nodded. He stood and made his way toward the sitting room door.

He had only just touched the door's handle when from behind him Lahr said, "Although . . ."

Don't say anything, Tilton told himself. *Pretend you haven't heard. Keep walking. Return to your life.*

"Although what?" he heard his voice say.

"There's another place you might try," came the voice softly from behind him. "Just in case . . ."

Tilton turned around, stared.

"Not that I'd recommend it," said Lahr, giving a shrug. Still slight, though less feeble than yesterday. "But up to you."

Another archive. That same disconnection: arriving almost before he knew he'd left Lahr's. That same sense that no matter what he said or did things would proceed inexorably, as they were meant to proceed. As if he had said the right thing, done the right thing. If *right* was the correct word.

This time the archive wasn't in a public facility but in a private mansion beyond a spiked gate. He climbed the gate, tearing open a shirtsleeve on the way up and hurting his ankle in the drop to the ground below. He limped past a security guard who seemed, somehow, blissfully unaware of him.

At the front door, he lifted a lion-headed clapper, let it bluntly fall.

Master Parkins was not at home, a butler told him, yet did not impede him from entering. Most rooms he tried were empty, but deep in the mansion an apparently wealthy man in a dressing gown, evidently Parkins, was seated beside a crackling fire.

"Good lord," the man said. "What the devil are you doing here? How did you get in?"

Tilton ignored the questions. Instead, he began to speak about the movie. *Desmond Parkins,* he suddenly knew the man's name to be, though he had no idea how. As Tilton talked, Parkins calmed down. Soon he loaded a pipe, smoked, listened.

"*Lather of Flies,* you say?" said Parkins. "Rather an odd title, that. You're sure you have it right, man?"

"I'm sure," said Tilton.

"And Lahr, you said? Sure about that name as well?"

Tilton nodded.

The man sucked deep on his pipe. He held the smoke in his lungs long enough that Tilton began to wonder if it was only tobacco. Finally, he let it out.

"Ever occur to you you're in over your head?" Parkins asked.

"Yes," said Tilton. "Recently."

"Ah," said Parkins. "Good man." He stared into his pipe. "I don't recall anything by Lahr in our collection. Nor anything by such a title." He rang a bell, summoning the butler. "Ah, Jenkins," he said. "*Lather of Flies.* Ring a bell?"

"No sir," said Jenkins.

"Thought not," said Parkins. He turned toward Tilton. "There, you see? I can do nothing for you."

Why was he so tired? It was not mere exhaustion, though it was that as well. It was as if some of the life of him, some vital essence, had leaked out.

"No luck again?" asked Lahr. He seemed to Tilton an entirely different man. Strong, robust, younger. He was out of his chair, pacing from one side of the room to the other, his stride confident. *What is happening?* wondered Tilton.

"No luck," he said.

"Too bad," said Lahr. "But, well, we expected as much, no? At least now we know it's not there. Still, let me think. Perhaps there is another, a third archive that I can suggest . . ."

"Describe it to me," Tilton managed, despite the fact his jaws seemed to want to say something else.

"Excuse me?" said Lahr, sharply. "Describe the archive? Why?"

But Tilton found he couldn't say anything to clarify. He stood there, helpless, gawping like a fish.

"The movie you must mean," Lahr prompted. *"Lather of Flies."*

Tilton nodded.

"Are you certain you want me to describe it to you?"

But by now Tilton not only couldn't answer, he couldn't move.

Some time had passed. Tilton wasn't sure how long. Maybe a few seconds, maybe much, much longer. He still couldn't move. Lahr was slowly circling him, watching him, attentive.

"How am I to describe it?" Lahr finally said. He came a little closer, stooped so his eyes were level with Tilton's. *"Lather of Flies.* Don't you think by now you're nearly as familiar with it as I am?"

Help me, thought Tilton.

Lahr came closer still. "Describe it?" Lahr said. "Oh, but *this* is the film, Tilton, if that really is your name. You've been in it all along. Not for your whole life, naturally, but ever since your encounter with

Serno." Lahr smiled. "Such an improbable name," he said, with contempt. "The kind of name found only in movies or books. Shouldn't that have given the game away?"

Still Tilton could do nothing. Couldn't speak, couldn't move.

"No film to be found," said Lahr softly. "But *lived* is a different matter. Though *lived* is not the right word, exactly." Lahr came closer still, until Tilton could see only part of his face. "Let's instead say you are one of the privileged few allowed to experience it. What luck for you." And even though Tilton could only see a smaller and smaller part of Lahr's face, he could tell from the man's voice, if it was a man, that Lahr was smiling.

And then Lahr straightened, stepped back, and slowly resumed his place in the wingback chair. He let his head fall lazily back against the soiled antimacassar. He mimed being feeble but, Tilton could tell from his eyes, he was not feeble at all. No, judging by those eyes, he was almost unbearably strong.

"Shall we go on to the next reel? It's quite something," said Lahr, the excitement of his voice belying his collapsed posture. "Unlike myself, I'm sorry to have to tell you, you won't make it to the very end of the film, though we'll have fun until then." And then, slowly, he smiled. "Or one of us will, anyway."

Still, Tilton could not move. He was no longer certain he could even breathe.

"Ready?" said Lahr. "And . . . action."

Acknowledgments

I would like to express my thanks to the Guggenheim Foundation for its invaluable support.

I would like to thank as well the editors of the following publications in which these stories appeared:

"No Matter Which Way We Turned": *People Holding.* Reprinted in Ellen Datlow, ed., *The Best Horror of the Year, Vol. 9.* Reprinted in Ellen Datlow, ed., *The Best of the Best Horror of the Year: Ten Years of Essential Short Horror.*
"Born Stillborn": *Catapult*
"Leaking Out": Mark Morris, ed., *New Fears 2*
"Song for the Unraveling of the World": *Bourbon Penn*
"The Second Door": Justin Steele and Sam Cowan, eds., *Looming Low.* Reprinted in Robert Shearman and Michael Kelly, eds., *Year's Best Weird Fiction, Vol. 5.*
"Sisters": Ellen Datlow and Lisa Morton, eds., *Haunted Nights*
"Room Tone": *The Masters Review*
"Shirts and Skins": *Hunger Mountain*
"The Tower": *Plinth*
"The Hole": Scott Dwyer, ed., *Phantasm/Chimera*

"A Disappearance": *Lake Effect*
"The Cardiacs": *Diagram*
"Smear": *Conjunctions.* Reprinted in John Joseph Adams and
   Charles Yu, eds., *The Best American Science Fiction and
   Fantasy, 2017.*
"The Glistening World": *Outlook Springs*
"Wanderlust": *Mississippi Review*
"Lord of the Vats": Scott Gable and C. Dombrowski, eds.,
   Ride the Star Wind
"Glasses": Ellen Datlow, ed., *Children of Lovecraft*
"Menno": *Gamut*
"Line of Sight": Michael Kelly, ed., *Shadows & Tall Trees 7*
"Trigger Warnings": *Autre Lettres*
"Kindred Spirit": *Lumina*
"Lather of Flies": Max Booth III and Lori Michelle, eds.,
   Lost Films

LITERATURE
is not the same thing as
PUBLISHING

Coffee House Press began as a small letterpress operation in 1972 and has grown into an internationally renowned nonprofit publisher of literary fiction, essay, poetry, and other work that doesn't fit neatly into genre categories.

Coffee House is both a publisher and an arts organization. Through our *Books in Action* program and publications, we've become interdisciplinary collaborators and incubators for new work and audience experiences. Our vision for the future is one where a publisher is a catalyst and connector.

Funder Acknowledgments

Coffee House Press is an internationally renowned independent book publisher and arts nonprofit based in Minneapolis, MN; through its literary publications and *Books in Action* program, Coffee House acts as a catalyst and connector—between authors and readers, ideas and resources, creativity and community, inspiration and action.

Coffee House Press books are made possible through the generous support of grants and donations from corporations, state and federal grant programs, family foundations, and the many individuals who believe in the transformational power of literature. This activity is made possible by the voters of Minnesota through a Minnesota State Arts Board Operating Support grant, thanks to the legislative appropriation from the Arts and Cultural Heritage Fund. Coffee House also receives major operating support from the Amazon Literary Partnership, the Jerome Foundation, McKnight Foundation, Target Foundation, and the National Endowment for the Arts (NEA). To find out more about how NEA grants impact individuals and communities, visit www.arts.gov.

Coffee House Press receives additional support from the Elmer L. & Eleanor J. Andersen Foundation; the David & Mary Anderson Family Foundation; Bookmobile; Fredrikson & Byron, P.A.; Dorsey & Whitney LLP; the Fringe Foundation; Kenneth Koch Literary Estate; the Knight Foundation; the Matching Grant Program Fund of the Minneapolis Foundation; Mr. Pancks' Fund in memory of Graham Kimpton; the Schwab Charitable Fund; Schwegman, Lundberg & Woessner, P.A.; the Silicon Valley Community Foundation; and the U.S. Bank Foundation.

The Publisher's Circle of Coffee House Press

Publisher's Circle members make significant contributions to Coffee House Press's annual giving campaign. Understanding that a strong financial base is necessary for the press to meet the challenges and opportunities that arise each year, this group plays a crucial part in the success of Coffee House's mission.

Recent Publisher's Circle members include many anonymous donors, Suzanne Allen, Patricia A. Beithon, the E. Thomas Binger & Rebecca Rand Fund of the Minneapolis Foundation, Andrew Brantingham, Robert & Gail Buuck, Dave & Kelli Cloutier, Louise Copeland, Jane Dalrymple-Hollo & Stephen Parlato, Mary Ebert & Paul Stembler, Kaywin Feldman & Jim Lutz, Chris Fischbach & Katie Dublinski, Sally French, Jocelyn Hale & Glenn Miller, the Rehael Fund-Roger Hale/Nor Hall of the Minneapolis Foundation, Randy Hartten & Ron Lotz, Dylan Hicks & Nina Hale, William Hardacker, Randall Heath, Jeffrey Hom, Carl & Heidi Horsch, the Amy L. Hubbard & Geoffrey J. Kehoe Fund, Kenneth & Susan Kahn, Stephen & Isabel Keating, Julia Klein, the Kenneth Koch Literary Estate, Cinda Kornblum, Jennifer Kwon Dobbs & Stefan Liess, the Lambert Family Foundation, the Lenfestey Family Foundation, Joy Linsday Crow, Sarah Lutman & Rob Rudolph, the Carol & Aaron Mack Charitable Fund of the Minneapolis Foundation, George & Olga Mack, Joshua Mack & Ron Warren, Gillian McCain, Malcolm S. McDermid & Katie Windle, Mary & Malcolm McDermid, Sjur Midness & Briar Andresen, Maureen Millea Smith & Daniel Smith, Peter Nelson & Jennifer Swenson, Enrique & Jennifer Olivarez, Alan Polsky, Marc Porter & James Hennessy, Robin Preble, Alexis Scott, Ruth Stricker Dayton, Jeffrey Sugerman & Sarah Schultz, Nan G. & Stephen C. Swid, Kenneth Thorp in memory of Allan Kornblum & Rochelle Ratner, Patricia Tilton, Joanne Von Blon, Stu Wilson & Melissa Barker, Warren D. Woessner & Iris C. Freeman, and Margaret Wurtele.

For more information about the Publisher's Circle and other ways to support Coffee House Press books, authors, and activities, please visit www.coffeehousepress.org/pages/support or contact us at info@coffeehousepress.org.